I0461502

WOLFGANG

BOOK 2

BEWARE OF THE FOBY

Will Lorimer

This book is a work of fiction. Authors, characters, businesses, organisations, places, events, and incidents, are imaginary. Any resemblance to actual persons, living or dead, is entirely coincidental.

Copyright © Will Lorimer

ISBN (print) 9789112789555

INKISTAN
.COM

The erstwhile Laird was running a coffee shop, 'Strictly half an hour,' his mate had promised when he left him in charge of 'Caffeinated Contentment™'. Empty then, the place was now filling up with regulars desperate for their early morning fix. As a barista, Wolfgang was a complete failure, even though he was giving his all. He knew the general terms, beyond the basic black & white and instant of his parents, but what the difference was between a cappuccino *wet* and *dry* he hadn't the remotest idea? Then there were the new expresso sub-divisions. So far, he had been asked for a *lungo, a quad* and a *no fun*, and he suspected there would be a lot more. Likewise, Americano, which now he learned could be *double tall, doppio, flat white, half-cut, skinny, half and half* and *with legs*. And that wasn't even including the confusingly named muffins, glowing like radioactive space debris in the illuminated glass counter display. So hazardous, apparently, a hairnet and protective gloves, were de rigueur and surgical steel tongs required to dole them out. Never mind the *honey buns, stroop waffles, salt donuts, jam beignets, raspberry croissants, almond biscotti* and *strüdel poodles,* in a separate compartment (also illuminated)- and dispensed with sterilised pincers. Ice cream had similar precautions, and was served in scalloped dollops, which looked quite small to his eyes, for all the portions were described as *super-sized*. There was an electronic till with a display with luminous little pictures of the above that responded to his finger. Everyone had cards instead of cash, or black devices they waved at the till which somehow charged for their order. What the fuck? He was only doglegging it in Wales, following a forking path traced on his 4d map reader, on route to meet up with his Inuit amanuensis, and resume dictating his novel, but instead he was running a coffee shop.

Five years refurbishing a castle in the remote wilds of the Kingdom and the World had clearly moved on. Who were these people? His last time in this Welsh hill town they were either scrawny sheep farmers subsidised by the RU, or malnourished hippies hiding away from the apocalypse subsisting on benefits and beans, not these branded types, sporting soft clothing bearing the slogans of organizations, nations and penal regimes Wolfgang had never heard of, with wires dangling from white buds in their ears. Neither were there any ashtrays, or indeed any smokers unless he counted two puffing away outside. It was a puzzle. What was this *lifestyle*, so prominently featured on the glossy cover of the 'Caffeinated Contentment™' brand magazines scattered about? Exactly how did that differ from a life? And what were all those devices they were intently tapping, collectively sounding like an insect colony. Were they beaming electronic messages, invisibly through the air? Perhaps not so invisibly, Wolfgang reconsidered, out the corner of his eye catching a glimpse of zipping trails shimmering in the smoke free Welsh air, reminding him of the fox fire he would sometimes see, coursing the strings, late at night working on his map of ley lines back at the castle. Only when he squinted, these luminous strings, though faint, were actually evident in day light, and seemed to be converging on the radio mast on the hill top, framed in the window of the cafe.

Amazing the changes, he considered with a shudder, trying not to focus on the busy lines of data crossing the room, some no doubt streaming through his innards, that very moment. To distract himself from obsessing over which vital organ the electronic messages might be messing with, he turned his attention back to the clientele, lounging on their sofas like snooty Lords and Ladies in a select club for the Gentry or perched on stools hunched at the high tables, which anyway hardly merited the term, being more like flat-backed cockroaches on attenuated legs reflected in the deep gloss of the specially imported African lignum vitae floorboards which showed up every spec of dirt and squashed jam muffin under the cockroach tables. That all being the general style of the so-called design ethic of Caffeinated Contentment™, as the manager, a former employee at the castle had explained, before running out of the door to answer a 'call', which Wolfgang suspected was not one of nature brought on by his double tall skinny mocha, for he had noticed there was a toilet in the back of the coffee shop, (disconcertingly for *both* sexes!) but rather was a telephone call on his mate's black device, which had chimed exactly like Big Ben striking the hour before he left so hurriedly. It was almost as disconcerting as learning of the latest unpleasant murder the day he hurriedly departed the

Castle, after signing a pre-divorce agreement, negotiated by Jaws his lawyer, on whom he was now dependant on funds. Only just making it over before the border was closed, reduced to driving a second-hand banger, which had broken down, not long after he crossed into in Wales.

Fortunately however, a couple of nice regulars – girls actually, who disconcertingly referred to themselves as 'guys', had taken pity on Wolfgang, and were helping out behind the counter making the intricacies of the expresso machine look easy, which had not been the case when Wolfgang had hardly been able to see the first customers for gusts of steam, as he pulled at the levers like a demented church organist playing a Bach fugue to a congregation of the damned. As it was the mid-morning rush of caffeine heads from new businesses which, since Wolfgang's last visit, had popped up like hallucinations brought on by magic mushrooms in the formerly boarded shops of the high street, selling windsurfing gear, scented soaps, gastronomic consumables - craft cheese, leek beer and such like, queuing for coffee *to go*, (another new term on Wolfgang) was snaking out the door, (which confusingly was opened by depressing a pad at the side) where there seemed to be some sort of disturbance with the smokers.

Wolfgang felt a nudge on his arm from Rachel, one of the girl/guys, at his side, who he now understood he was supposed to think of as his co-worker, behind the counter.

'I think you better go help old Nick.' She pointed one of her star speckled fingernails, at the door, 'that's him just outside. He's always complaining about something,' she shrugged, smiling sweetly. 'But it takes all kinds, dunnit.'

Can I help you sir,' Wolfgang said, smiling insincerely down at the lanky man folded into the electric assisted wheelchair, who appeared to be a recent convert to the new order sweeping rural Wales, his greying hair pulled back in a lank pony tail, hanging over the astrakhan collar of his smart tweed jacket, which was unbuttoned, and clearly a new purchase, unlike his worn yellow waistcoat, stained green corduroy trousers, and scuffed brown brogues, the laces undone on one shoe.

'About time,' he snarled, looking up, 'can't you café fiend people do something about that bloody ramp.'

'What's wrong with it? Wolfgang enquired with genuine curiosity, since he associated shop doorways with steps, and wanted to know more.

'Too steep for the servos of my new e-zippy,' The man said, tapping a gloved driving hand to the battery of his sleek electric wheel chair, which appeared to have been designed in a wind tunnel. 'This disabled access is borderline illegal.'

'Sorry to hear that Sir. Assuredly, I will pass your complaint on to the management,' Wolfgang lied, since he had no intention of doing so, wondering how a perfectly functional doorway could, at the same time, be borderline disabled *and* illegal, as he smoothly steered the wheelchair past the queue.

'Stop here!' The man ordered abruptly, waving towards the toilet area at the back of the shop. 'Park the e-zippy there, when you are ready, I'll have a half and half mocha and organic Alvera sweetener, with a buttered malted toasty, crème cheese and a slice of lime on the side. I'll be in my usual place,' he pointed to a sagging yellow sofa, which fortunately was unoccupied.

'But won't you need your wheel chair? Wolfgang asked, restraining an urge to stuff the grumpy old fart back down into his seat, as he rose from it.

'In case you were wondering, I am not disabled,' the man, who was surprisingly tall, said drawing himself up haughtily, and looking down his flute of a nose at Wolfgang, 'Just vertically challenged, that's all.'

Yes, it was a rude awakening to a very changed world out-with the Kingdom, Wolfgang had in the heartlands in Wales, but a good preparation for his arrival in the big city where his amanuensis impatiently awaited him. The castle, and the moonshine of a buccaneering past, fading in the mists of a Kingdom that time forgot, as the bright colours bled out on the tapestry that Brünhida wove after their marriage, and the shooting star which was supposed to represent him, plunged to earth, before emerging on the far side of the horizon into the brash light of this brand new day.

SESSION #1

Wolfgang resumed his surveillance of his amanuensis. Behind the raised lid of his expensive new laptop computer, with its double head eagle brand glowing evilly, she was filing her nails again. By rights, by now they should be stumps. Long even strokes, back and forth, back and forth, it was endless. Christ it was hypnotic. Rasp rasp. Like a woodman's saw, and about as long.

Where was he? French windows half open onto a small balcony, scattered with autumn leaves from trees outside. Below the Victorian scrollwork of the balcony's rusting balustrade, the red roof of a double decker bus going past. London then.

Closer, a low building across the road, slates slick with rain, the sky the same grey as the day he took occupancy, following a serendipitous encounter, a couple of miles away in the heart of the City.

Seven Dials had showed up green orange on his 4d map reading device, offering a confluence of possibilities, something he guessed was to do with the unusual configuration of seven cross roads. The fact it was the seventh day of the month, was another success indicator. A connection to Caffeinated Contentment™, back in Wales, albeit across the several centuries, was further suggested by a plaque above the basement doorway of the Three Cheers pub, which was on either the seventh or the first corner of the intersection, depending on which way he turned his forking schematic and adjusted the scale to fit the page of his London A-Z. According to the legend, the pub was the smallest in England, and occupied the site of the gentlemen's club where coffee was first drunk back in the 17th century. The name of the pub derived from the habit of the original doorman of shouting into the London fog, as the last three honourable members, finally staggered out of the club, 'three chairs, three chairs for the Gentlemen,' whereupon six footmen carrying three sedan chairs appeared from the surrounding streets, before the gentlemen went their separate ways, carried in their sedan chairs.

Sedan-chair.

Wolfgang was seated on one of only three reproduction sedan chairs, all the limited space of the dimly lighted basement pub would allow, when the only other customer, a tall gaunt man in a cashmere coat, pushing past his table, upset the erstwhile laird's drink. That led to Wolfgang graciously accepting another from the stranger who he took to be a property agent of some kind from the large bunch of keys jangling at his waist, inside his unbuttoned cashmere coat. But there was more, when he returned from the bar, and leaned in, to set down the glasses on the table, his broad shoulders looming over the lamp seemed to spread bat wings, before he sat down in the sedan chair opposite.

Wolfgang got a glimpse of gold in a half-cracked grin as the man introduced himself, 'every wune knows me round heah, as Plain John,' he laughed, 'that's because Oi'm such a pain, when you geyt to know me.' He smiled, almost threateningly, 'three cheahs,' he said, raising his pint glass. 'Heah's mud in your eyes, cock!'

'And in yours,' Wolfgang rejoindered, not sure if he had just been insulted.

Done for introductions, Plain John went on, plain as plain, explaining he was in need of distraction from disquieting news he had received about his boss.

'Serious?' Wolfgang raised an eyebrow.

'With the amount involved, I recon sow.' Plain John nodded. 'Roight now, 'e's on trial mate, yea, on trial,' he nodded again, as if confirming the matter to himself, 'for embezzlement, that's wot.'

'At the Old Bailey?' Wolfgang immediately sensed a high stakes court drama, from the man's plain tone.

'Na, sumwheah else,' Plain John shook his head.

'Moscow?' Wolfgang hazarded, suspecting that Plain John's employer was a wealthy foreign national.

'You got it in one, mate, got it in one.' Reaching a hand into the breast pocket of his coat, Plain John glanced up at the no smoking sign above the empty bar, cracked the cellophane of the cigarette pack with a practiced broad thumb that might have belonged to a strangler, disposed of the foil with a flick, drew an untipped cigarette and lit it with a gold Dupont lighter.'

Help yourself mate,' he said, waving a meaty hand and a clutch of rings, not plain at all, at the open pack on the table, took a deep draw on his cigarette, settled back in his sedan chair, his exhalation, expanding like a UFO settling down over the table lamp between them, the blue smoke casting a spooky glow over the proceedings.

'Care to 'ear a story, mate?' he said, under the hood of the sedan chair, his eyes shining like two coins in the darkness. Gold or brass, it was hard to tell.

'Got all afternoon if it's a good one,' the author replied from the shadows of his chair.

It was a long story, with few salient details, in the telling, but all the more interesting for it, when Wolfgang learned of the recently vacated, terraced house that needed 'warming', one of several properties owned by a Russian oligarch currently on trial in Moscow charged with embezzlement of billions of roubles from state funds. Owed for back wages, and left in charge of the properties, the upshot Plain John clearly was embittered and didn't foresee his former employer returning to London any time soon.

'A hundred nicker', in the form of two crisp £50 notes, passed under the table, an underhand move Wolfgang felt was expected, but thought unnecessary - given the barman was outside clearing the tables on the street. Anyone that asks, he is to say he is the caretaker, but no names, can be mentioned. Wolfgang understands exactly, and understands nothing. Sitting in a red Alpha Romeo coupe, that is anything but plain, parked outside a terraced Victorian townhouse, Plain John hands over the key to the front door, says he might pop by once in a while, for some 'fings' he keeps in a basement locker, but apart from that Wolfgang is free to use all the rooms. Plain John is pleased, and writes down the number of his *'Dog and bone'*, which Wolfgang understands to mean his black telephone device he keeps in his coat breast pocket, which Plain John says he is only to call from a phone box, *and only in case of emergencies*. He adds he is busy and probably won't not pop by for a while, which is ok by Wolfgang. They shake hands then Plain John drives off in his Alpha Romeo car towards the traffic lights of Hackney Road.

Though not up to the accommodation of the castle, Wolfgang was more than satisfied, despite the questionable plumbing, the unfamiliar Russian electric sockets, the cracked tiles above the sunken marble bath in the bathroom, the box of used dildoes and packets of condoms he'd found in a cupboard below the stairs, the cheap chrome trim and plastic surfaces of the kitchen, the smells of talcum powder and patchouli, pervading the 4 bedrooms, and the red satin sheets on the beds, the chunky Russian furniture of steel and concrete, cluttering the two reception rooms. Most impressive was the garage excavated in the foundations, entered from the lane at the back, which he thought would make an excellent workshop, should he get one of his inspirations in the middle of the night.

Becoming aware he had been drifting again, careful not to trip the spin switch again, Wolfgang swivelled his electrically assisted Sputnik executive chair around to face the *baggage* again, 'Where were we?' he asked her.

'*You* were trying to remember a session from those typescripts your Jew boy pal stole.'

'That was never him.'

'What was his real name?'

Wolfgang frowned, then remembered, 'Charles Ivor Goldfink. But after university he changed his surname by deed poll ...'

'No wonder.' She interjected.

'Called himself Kafka. Actually, he really believed he was a reincarnation of the famous writer.' Wolfgang chuckled.

'Such self-serving delusional bullshit is typical of his kind. He certainly had you fooled.'

Wolfgang shook his head, 'Of all those who passed through the castle, only he stayed loyal.'

'Don't you believe it,' she laughed. 'He played you like a violin, off against your wife.'

'Just what have you got against him?' Wolfgang sat up in his Sputnik chair.

'Apart from those papers he stole?'

Deciding not to challenge her last remark, Wolfgang shrugged.

'I hate verminous forms of life – especially cockroaches,' she snarled.

He sighed, knowing there was no way to change her Boreal supremacist views, considering as she did all people south of Arctic Circle racially inferior, to those above it – and of those, most *especially Inuits.* 'Where were we?'

'*You* were talking about one of the missing typescripts.'

'Which series?' he yawned.

'The sleep deprivation stories.'

'Can you recall the title?

ZaZa frowned spectacularly.

'Just the title?' he pleaded through the amnesiac fogs of his last spliffette, which necessarily had been a single skinner because he was running low on hash.

'Wolfgang, must I remind you again I am only here to type what you dictate. Any other services, are strictly out-with the bounds of our new contract.'

'Did you say *new* contract?'

'It's the standard form, issued by the RAS.'

'What's that?' Wolfgang interrupted.

'A professional trade body which looks after the interests of Amanuenses. The R means Royal, for your information, since the Monarch takes a close interest in the affairs of our society.'

'I bet she does.'

'He, Wolfgang, *he*,' ZaZa repeated, 'She, as we were endlessly told at the time, passed on to higher reams, ages ago.

Now, come over here, I have just pulled the contract up on the screen if you care to have a look.'

'But I don't see any mention of porridge?' he said, standing peering over her shoulder.

'Wolfgang,' she responded testily, 'I have no need for any more, as you will insist on calling it, *porridge.*'

'I have been meaning to ask what you plan doing withit? You must have quarts by now.'

'That's my business!' she snapped, 'Sufficient to say I have enough of your cum stored for my purposes now.'

'I wish you wouldn't call it that.' Wolfgang shuddered, wondering again what evil designs his Inuit secretary had on his testicular porridge –no doubt now stored in an igloo north of the

55th degree of latitude – Sperm he thought of as his *golden oaties*, though only occasional having golden flecks as they discovered in the Institute, where he was detained before he escaped. 'So how much am I supposed to pay you?'

ZaZa pointed a lurid green fingernail.

'What?' he exclaimed, peering at the screen, 'that's outrageous. How am I supposed to come up with such a sum every week?'

'Wolfgang that is not much more than what you would have to pay an agency for an average typing temp. Which, must I remind you, I am anything but!' she said, looking really quite indignant.

'ZaZa, don't you understand, I'm practically skint.'

'With a town house on the edge of the City, a marble bathroom out of a movie, a designer kitchen, this,' she gestured, at the plush red drapes, framing the french windows, her oversized finger pointing out the cherubs of the fake cornices, and the sputnik furniture below, '*And* the garage in the basement you *still* haven't shown me?' She shook her head, incredulously. 'Listen Wolfgang *practically skint* in this city, gets you a shop doorway, or park bench at best.'

'I got it cheap, and you can't say this is a good area, with those burned out car wrecks in the Council housing scheme round the corner and the sunk barge in the Grand Union Canal, by the park.'

'Wolfgang this new pad of yours has to be worth at least five million.'

'I rather doubt that,' he said, deciding to keep schtum on how he came by it. Otherwise she would extract information on his 4d map reading device and its applications which, he had only just begun to grasp, were manifold. Besides, she knew far too much about him already.

'Wolfgang, I couldn't afford to rent a cupboard this near the City not even with Skull paying for it.'

'You're with Skull again?' He squeaked, his sphincter retracting instantly, upon realizing the two halves of the nightmare team were back together, with all that implied.

'Yes,' she smiled silkily, 'And what a good boy he's been.'

Wolfgang grimaced, 'I find that hard to imagine.'

'His new business is doing very well.'

'And what is that?' he growled.

'Landscape gardening in the suburbs where we are forced to live at the end of the tube line, not being privately funded as you so obviously still are, despite your denials.'

She looked at her watch, as in the distance a church bell rang the half hour, 'Now, we have exactly twenty nine minutes, and forty one seconds left of our session today. Are you going to dictate something, or must I resume sharpening my nails again?'

THE GLORY AND THE ECSTASY

by Diogenes C. Horse.

I *was wrapped in a black sack lying on a hospital bed. How had this come about? I'd known the headbanger, otherwise herein referred to as Melon, for years but only from a* distance ...

'Wolfie...?'

'What?' the erstwhile Laird growled, irritated beyond measure by this latest interruption - *and just when he was getting going ...*

'Don't worry, I'll add in an extra minute at the end of the session.'

'You'd better,' Wolfgang scowled back at her.

'I only want to know, what does the initial "C" stand for?'

'That's for the reader to guess.'

'But I am your amanuensis, surely I have a right to know?'

'You have no rights other than what is stated in our contract.

'Please Wolfgang,' she made a face, reminding him of a photo he'd once seen of a baby seal, poking up through a hole in Arctic ice.

'I would have thought it was obvious,' he said, wishing he had a harpoon to hand.

'I promise to keep it a secret.' She raised two oversized, crossed fingers. 'Honestly.'

'I'll tell you when we get to that allotted minute at the end, and not before.'

'Wolfgang, you are so mean.'

'And you are an untrustworthy Inuit racist undeserving of my porridge.'

... I came across Melon again a couple of years before Anne and I married and moved into her ancestral home ...

'Wolfie?'

'Goddamnit, ZaZa, what is it now?' Wolfgang roared.

'An important point of continuity! But if you don't want to know, that's Ok.'

'Alright then, tell me,' Wolfgang's eyes bulged with the effort of retaining his overheated cerebrum which was threatening to explode his nasal passages.

'I thought you moved into the castle immediately after you married.'

'We did.'

'That's not what you just dictated.'

'So?' he shrugged.

'But why is she now called Anne?'

'Because I am sick of the name Brünhilda. Anyway, this is dictated by a different author, the eponymous Diogenese c. Horse, in case you hadn't noticed. Certain details are bound to have changed.'

'Perhaps you should issue a mental health warning to the readers.'

'Why, for god's sake?'

'In case someone sues you for brain damage.'

'Perhaps I will contact a temp typing agency after all.' Wolfgang muttered, clutching his head.

'Haven't you noticed, Wolfie? These days health warnings are everywhere,' she said, reaching into the breast pocket of her denim shirt, and brandishing a cigarette packet, 'Look they even have pictures of cancerous lungs from autopsies. Isn't that gross?'

'Oh my god,' Wolfgang clutched his neck, as in the distance a church bell rang the hour, reminding him of oranges and lemons, *and* the bells of St Clements which, in the old nursery song, ring out when the king gets his head chopped off. "The world really has changed. I should never have left the Kingdom.'

'So why did you?'

'Do what?' he blinked.

'Leave the Kingdom? You're like a fish out of water away from your castle,' she said, checking her watch. 'There it is, your extra minute.' She rose from her seat, 'You can tell me why Anne and not Brünhilda next session Wolfie, this one is over. But before I go, tell me what does that initial C in the new author's name stand for?'

'What do you think?

'I don't know,' she said, her evil Inuit face a mask of innocence.

'Cunt!' Wolfgang said disingenuously, pointing to the door. 'And leave the laptop on the Louis XIV, please. I paid for it.'

'But you don't know anything about computers.'

'I am well acquainted with their operation.'

'Like when?' she said, as if the point mattered.' 'They don't have any in your backwards Kingdom.

'They do in the R.U. Economic Border Zone. I often looked over the shoulders of people operating them on them on my trips down here.'

'I heard you need a special pass to get in.'

'Like checkpoints would stop me.' he snorted, derisively.

'So, what was in those packages you brought back?'

'You saw them?' Wolfgang was appalled.

'Yes, I watched you returning from the Zone, and that factory you would never talk of. When you thought no one was looking sneaking those boxes out of the boot of your heap of a car, that you claimed was vintage and said was perfect for your nefarious night time missions, but to me the car looked like a

wreck you had just pulled out of a pond, and that's the real reason you were never checked.'

'You saw me?' Wolfgang was aghast.

'Yes,' more icicles in her grin than a Boreal cat looking out an igloo, 'sneaking past the Airstream, keeping to the shadows, tip toeing the gravel round the side of the Tower to the boiler room door. Then your shadow in the stained-glass window in the tower that you stole from your old school, creeping up the stairs to the Clock Room, which you always kept locked.'

'For a good reason,' he laughed. 'If anyone's sneaky it's you.'

'Wolfgang, when you are like this, it unsettles the balance of our professional relationship.'

'How?'

'Sub-clause 4 of Article 23 of our contract, I'll show you.' She flipped open the contentious lap top on the table, and in a flurry of oversized fingers typed in a string of letters and numbers, which showed as a line of dots in a box that appeared on the screen.

'What's that?' he asked, pointing around her shoulder.

'The password. You need that to get in.' She scowled as only an Inuit can, 'I thought you said you knew about computers.'

'I counted fourteen strokes.' he grinned slyly, wiggling his eyebrows.

'Thirteen actually,' she countered. 'The fourteenth was the enter key.' She indicated with an outsize finger. 'There, your first lesson.' She turned the lap top around as a page appeared on the screen, headed:

MEMORANDUM OF AGREEMENT:

'Please note Sub-Clause 4 here.' she tapped the screen, impatiently. 'I'll read it out, since you seem to be needing glasses. *"Applying to Agreements between Dictators (party A) and Dictatees. (party B) Withholding by A to B may be considered to constitute a breach of contract, with all the said penalties that apply in such a judgement."'*

'So, what does that mean?'

'Wolfgang, as party B I have legal rights.'

'And responsibilities ...'

Yes,' she nodded, 'one of which is to remind you withholding is a serious matter.'

'I'll get to that story, I promise. For now, I just want to learn how to work that computer. I am not planning to replace you, honestly.'

'Wolfgang you can play all you want on it after I have removed some files from it.'

'Just leave it here, so I can practice over the weekend.' He raised a finger, 'Remember, I paid for it.'

'I grant you that, so ok.' she grimaced, 'but you'll only be able to access the Imp tutorial programs. This computer is password protected and you won't get past mine.'

'It looked complicated.'

Her eyes narrowed.

'7S couldn't break it, so don't even think about trying.'

'What's that?'

'The Seventh Son.' ZaZa frowned, 'it's a super computer in Californica.'

'Californica?' Wolfgang raised an eyebrow, 'As in the Fornicating state?' He laughed.

'California, as everyone knows, seceded from the US last year after the 6 Day Data War, and is now Californica in the Greater Pacific Federation, which of course includes the United Boreal States of my free Inuit peoples.'

Baffled, he shook his head, 'It's the first I've heard of any of that.'

'Really Wolfgang, that's old news!' She rolled her eyes, 'Don't you know anything? Where have you been?'

'Too long in the Kingdom it seems,' he sighed. 'Apparently, a year in the land that time forgot amounts to at least five elsewhere,' Wolfgang said ruefully, wondering how this recent Data War and the new world alignment had escaped him. 'Please, at least explain why is this super computer called the Seventh Son?'

'Because it's the seventh generation Max Mind, and the fastest QI yet, capable of processing 16 quadrillion petaflops of data simultaneously. It drives the SuperInk Network.'

And that is?' Wolfgang said, not risking exposing his ignorance further, by asking what QI and petaflops meant.

'The SuperInk Economy. Get a life! Wolfgang you've got a lot to catch up if you wish to be a contender again.'

'Thanks for that,' Wolfgang looked back up at her from his sputnik chair, 'I still am, by the way.'

'Whatever,' she laughed, holding up an outsize hand, while buttoning up her fluffy white Inuit coat with the other, 'Don't get up, you look too comfortable in that chair. I'll let myself out. See you after the weekend. Till then.' She waved at the laptop computer, open on the Louis XIV desk between them. 'Practice all you want.'

Still laughing to herself, she closed the door of the first-floor room behind her, and disdaining the lift as usual proceeded quickly down the stairs, her heels clicking on the Siberian maple parquet of the entrance hall, before he heard the front door close behind her. Through the open balcony doors, the sound of her mirth continuing, even as the 49e bus, pulled up at the stop below, before driving off with the baggage on board.

ROACH here again ...

*C*aracas, 5th July, the Plaza Major Hotel, on the corner of *Bolivar Square, where tonight they are celebrating Venezuela's Independence Day yet again with tear gas and Molotov cocktails.*

A party which they tell me never ends in this socialist paradise, where I have been three weeks trying to track down Wolfgang's casket, on its route around the world on the UPS merry go

round, since the SuperInk network crashed during the third World Data War, when everyone lost their heads, before Big Brand took over and service was partially restored, last year.

Enough about my frustrations fulfilling the onerous duty, which the only reason I have for continuing living since Wolfgang died and a light went out of the world. I am sure that is what he would like me to say. However the search does relieve the tedium of a wandering existence, and my sentence to serve as witness to the follies of man, till the last trump sounds, when this reality is rolled up like a length of silk, and stored away in the great repository, or wherever all the bales are kept, away from the light that would fade the colours.

Light which burned all night at the Castle, that cold winter when everything froze, and the kitchen was the only heated room in the big house, where Wolfgang worked obsessively on his expanding map of string lines, which met at myriads of points around three walls, and when conditions were right, forked with fox fire. The pale strings coursing with phosphorescence when the aurora borealis flared in the crack between the window curtains, over the hill opposite. Not that he paid much attention, pacing back and forth, his face glowing green in the eldritch light of St Elmo, the patron saint of those who venture on the face of the deeps. Navigators like Wolfgang, going without sleep for days at a time, sailing into the 4th *dimension, measuring distances and plotting alignments at the big kitchen table. Only pausing to roll another joint, the harsh cry of a bittern echoing over the ghostly reedbeds of the icebound river, reminding Wolfgang he has lines to string and more pins to press, before Brünhilda descends to eat her oat wheaties, for breakfast, at her regular time of 10.30.*

It was in the false spring of the Great Cold, when the temperatures briefly rose in March, and for a few days we thought the record freeze was over. I had been cleaning out the stables where Lady Brünhilda's pet Alpacas were kept after she returned with a breeding pair following the wedding of a friend in Bolivia, and was crossing the slushy courtyard with my wheelbarrow filled with lovely steaming Andean poo, heading for the raised beds of the Veg garden, when the Laird on high leaned out of a 4th floor window of the Clock tower, and summoned me to up to his studio in the eves.

Expecting a rocket for another of my messes, instead I was regaled with an account of a realization he'd come to one hot summer afternoon, after correlating the fight paths of the wolf flies that plagued the Castle in the summer months, with the forking paths of the famous maze in the veg garden.

The fly on which he had lavished so much of the attention
he rarely gave to me, was a particularly top-heavy example of
the Wolf genus. It's rotor wings, so called because of their
markings were iridescent in sunlight, and appeared to spin.
Bigger than the other local flies, it seemed a wonder this
prodigious fly could defy gravity, let alone zip about, so fast
indeed, Wolfgang insisted, not I think disingenuously, that he
only had to blink, and it disappeared into a blue void, before
reappearing somewhere off, before once more he blinked, and
lost it again. Zip, zip, fork fork, went the fly on its little journey,
disappearing into the blue between triangulated points. And he
supposed that was the point, because the forks where it

reappeared and changed direction, served as stepping stones to the next energy point, or fork, where the cumbersome fly obviously recharged, otherwise how could it fly? The laws of aeronautics denied it, he claimed, and I could see he was sincere. Clearly, he went on, the triangulated points marked the junctures where the fourth dimension intruded into our world and into which his namesake flies flipped on their journeys. And as ever, so above, as above, Wolfgang continued, dyslexically, his neural pathways, obviously forking with his words, or so I imagined with my little cockroach mind.

I must admit that though he had lost me by then, such was his vehemence, I doubted not his sincerity for one second, a period I supposed was considerably longer in his sleep deprived state than it was for me. An observation kept to myself, for fear of being called a miserable cockroach, and having my carapace stamped on again, before being banished from his sight as so often before. Remembering this and other incidents, when I drew his ire, my mind wandered, and so I was surprised, when he crossed to a corner of his studio, and with a dramatic flourish whipped away the cloth covering what I had assumed to be a large packing crate, dramatically revealing his prototype map reading device.

Standing about four feet high, it had a viewing port with eyeholes at the top. Grinning wolfishly, he opened a door in the side, cranked a handle, and directed me to peer inside, and tell him what I see. Vaguely I made out gossamer threads pinned across of a descending series of frames, here and there dull glass beads, sliding erratically along the criss-cross lines, until he remembered to press a switch. Lights flickered and it seemed I was looking down through golden combs into a beehive, at the base of which was spread a map of the kingdom across which coloured lights played. As he cranked faster and faster, iridescent bugs slid and transited like hyper planets in space, or a four-way abacus, I couldn't decide. I admit I was entranced by what could be achieved with a packing case, some lights, simple threads, and coloured beads, all purchased for a few pounds in a bargain store in a country town. But then I am a Cockroach and what do I know.

Later, I composed a song, which began with the lines:

> *Snow gets under your chin-chin, in Sweden,*
> *But Turnips get in wellies in the Kingdom,*
> *Where undergarments are banned,*
> *And the length pf Kilts is rrregulated,*
> *And ventilated by icy blasts and hellish heat,*
> *Where Ladder are greased and*
> *Folk stand on rungs, look up bums,*
> *Grasp ankles, of those above*
> *And stamp on heads of those below.*

All play the game, except
The Laird of Haggard,
Up there in his high tower,
Says he's writing a book,
But I think its malfeasance
Against So-cie-te-he,
He's planning at his desk...
Tra la la ...

But I was careful to mumble that last part, to do so loudly, would have risked that ire I was always anxious to avoid, even if I did slip in sly asides referencing his antics in my lyrics. However, whereas I was but a simple fool, Wolfgang was anything but, as his prototype demonstrated. His madness always had method. And in its expression, somehow it always came out alright, though not without casualties, as is now clear.

Evidently, at least in part placated by my chitchitlin oo's and ah's of appreciation, but still not satisfied, he then urged me to empty my cockroach mind, and look again through the eyeholes at the top and tell me what I saw on the map.

'Lights, colours, green blue, shifting lines, dark light spots, and yes, and there, a fork too,' Lost for anything more to say, I added, brightly, as I hoped, 'I imagine, it takes some time, to get your eye in.'

Wolfgang scrutinised me suspiciously. 'Yes, it does, and when you do there is no end in view. But I guess even simple map reading is above your level, though you are welcome to try again.'

That warmed me, still I was uneasy to be the recipient of his affection, wondering what came next – the fire of his ire, or sit down share a couple of j's and a bit for a joint later, he was generous that way. I was never without from his table for long. I jest, but he certainly had a way with the crumbs of hash, over and above burrow and board. His to summon and dismiss, as he liked, which strangely, I wanted too. Never sure if I was a fagot or a cockroach after he caught me wanking in a bush, when I should have been painting the porch before the storms, which were always expected anytime soon. Thunder rolling over the brow of the hill, when he was around. You felt him *before he arrived, that's what I used to think, but never said, of course.*

Disappointed, but certainly not surprised at my lack of acuity, being that I was an execrable cockroach in his estimation, he covered the prototype up again with the cloth, and I was dismissed.

Imagine my surprise, several years later, during his period of exile, on my one visit to his Russian house in London, he showed me his much reduced and to my eyes remarkably improved 4-dimensional map reading device.

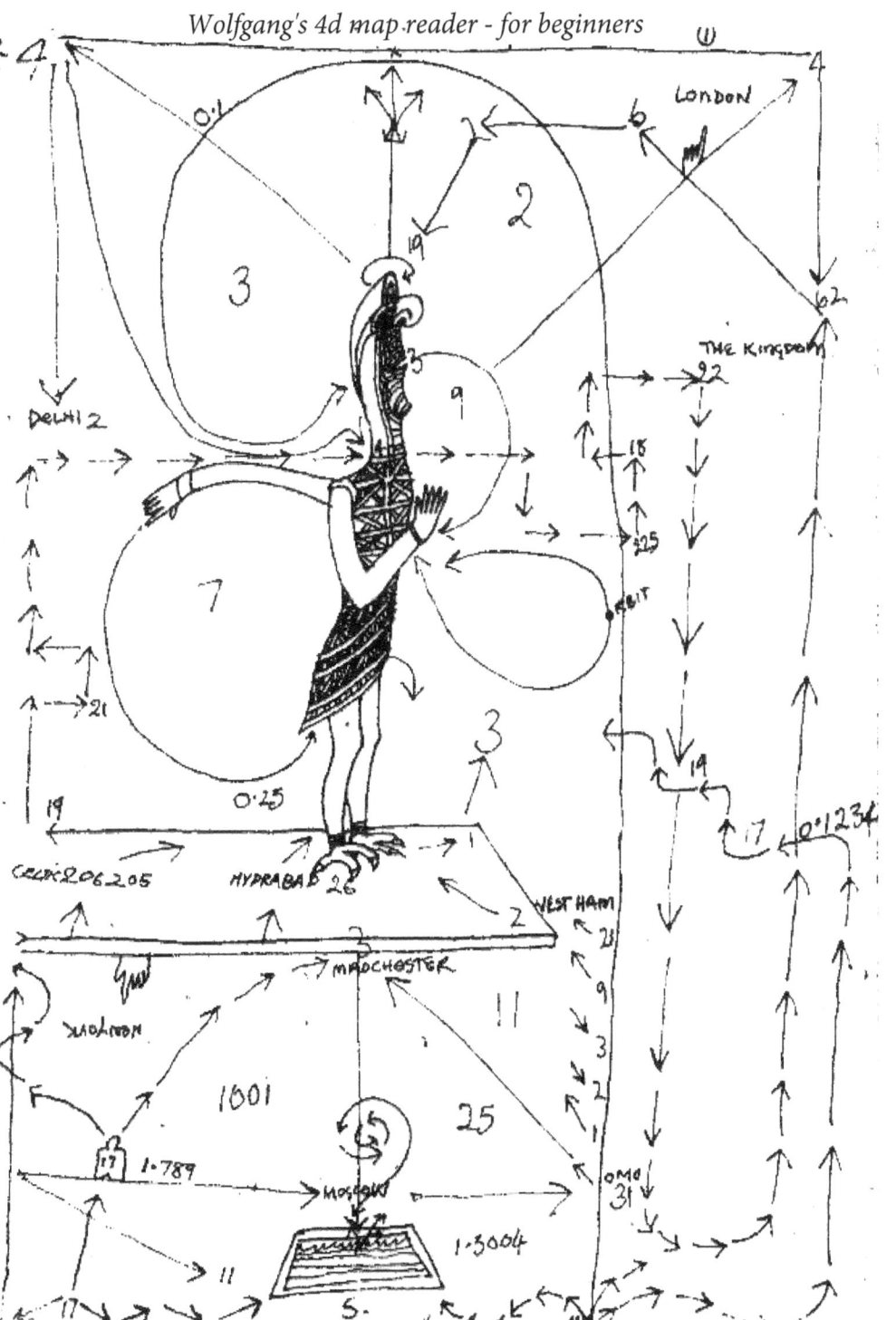

Laid on the open page of a standard London A-Z book and about the same size, the device consisted of a screen held in a metal frame. Twiddling a black knob precipitated colour changes on the map illuminated below. Whereas turning the red knob on the opposite side created moiré effects. Wolfgang explained that the filters within were coated with nano layers of rare metals, that had been extracted from meteorites, which refracted unearthly spectrums at polarizing angles. The filters were laser cut on one side with a repeat design of the maze of forking paths, which the Trappists precisely milled, repeating the schematics 440 times on the glass in lines .0001 of a micron across. Light passing between the reflective sides of the plates, was caught in the microscopic grooves between the forks, from where it shot out unearthly rays, scattering in a shining lattice of beams and shadows - Which he added, his tone darkening, was where the 4th dimension came in.

However, used as I was to his passionate declamations, knowing he could utter a contradictory opinion in the same sentence as easily as falling off a horse, the most interesting aspect of the device was the glass itself, which in typical devious fashion Wolfgang had obtained out of the back door of a secret weapons facility, in the special economic enterprise zone, between the R.U. Federation and the Kingdom, originally from a cleaner who worked nights in the factory. After she retired, Wolfgang introduced himself to the management and *threatened to inform the parent company, a mysterious Trappist corporation in America, of the ease with which he'd breeched their security, and so was granted privileged access. Existing as a closed sect within the Military Defence complex, the warrior monks were dedicated to defending Christendom, which one way or another they had been doing with their alchemical arts, for a nigh on thousand years. And the trichroic glass which the fourteenth abbot, Lord Raleigh, had invented in 1893, and which no one but a Trappist had ever succeeded in making since, was for deployment in space above the North and South Poles, where it was assembled into orbiting mirrors, waiting for the day when they would to redirect the energy from nuclear devices exploded nearby, against the enemy - on earth, the moon, or wherever they were located. I imagined how much Wolfgang would have enjoyed employing killer beams from space against his foes, who had proliferated before he was forced into exile from his beloved castle. But then Wolfgang always said there were ways and means. All one needed, apparently, was to adopt the right approach, and any problem, no matter how great, could be **neutralized.** Yes, that was the word he used, showing side of his character, which I hadn't seen before. But then what did I know, scurrying down the stairs with my crumb to the safety of my burrow, previously belonging to a mole.*

THE A-Z OF DIVINATION

No sooner had ZaZa left, Wolfgang was possessed by the notion it was vital that he discover her password on the laptop and investigate her files *before* she returned after the weekend. Indeed, he felt his life depended on cracking the code. Such instances were not uncommon, a sudden idea would take a hold, and he would not rest until he succeeded or reached the bitter end, when it became clear he must desist, or die in the attempt. This time it was no different. He was pretty sure the password was 14 characters long, despite her claim it was 13, and moreover that it included at least two X's, probably a S, possibly a Y or a U, but that was all he had come up with, recreating her flailing typing style, recapitulating the moment she entered the password, while in a trance induced by counting backward in Cantonese, a language he had a passing knowledge of, after purchasing a set of Master Wu's hypno-tapes, which he had found discounted in the bargain store in Snaresburgh, years before.

He had tried *Augury* as practiced in Ancient Rome, which involves studying the movements of birds, in his case watching the flight paths of pigeons over the rooftops across the road outside.

He would have attempted *Bibliomancy,* only he only didn't have a copy of the Bible handy, unless he counted the Russian Orthodox version in Cyrillic, which had turned up in a cupboard in the bathroom when he was rooting about for pills to fix a headache induced by password fever.

Likewise, *Brontomancy* for there had been no thunder over the city that weekend. *Cartomancy,* or divination by cards, was a proven method which had worked for him in the past, however, despite his efforts with a pack purchased in a brief foray to Cunning Lane market, and a rake of the second-hand stalls, after he was directed there, by his 4D map reader, nothing came up, probably because the pack was too new.

Neither was there any result from dowsing, dangling his signet ring over letters of the alphabet and the numbers 1-100, he'd written on the back of a menu in the Al-Majid Curry café, which opened its doors early on market days, where he had a very good biriyani, and a conversation with Ali, the Sufi proprietor, about summoning djinn, which got nowhere, because there wasn't time.

Eleomancy, which involved pouring oil on water, and swirling the mixture about with a finger, was visually interesting, but gave him nothing by way of numbers or letters. The fortune cookies that came with his Saturday night take-away from a nearby Chinese restaurant, informed him that his lucky colour was green, and he should pay attention to the number 6, but that was all.

He would have tried *fructomancy,* but the normally failsafe bananas at the morning market, were near enough spotless to render the attempt useless, while the apples appeared to have been sprayed with furniture polish by the cunning stall holder. All of them shone with a plastic sheen, none were wrinkled and deformed, or gargoyle like in appearance, as is ideal for the purposes of divination.

He had limited success with *Gastromancy* after purchasing two tins of baked beans but could make nothing from his burps and farts, after forcing himself to eat the contents.

He also tried *Hakata*, and divination by dice, assigning different letters to the faces of six dice, also purchased at the market, but though he came up with lots of combinations of 13 characters, nothing worked as a password, possibly because the dice were made of plastic, rather than ivory as was recommended – narwal ivory being ideal, of course.

Hydromancy, or scrying the ripples in a bucket of water, into which he dropped pebbles, as practiced by adepts in the Ashrams of Hyderabad in India, seemed less than useless, since all he saw were concentric circles, which after a while made him dizzy.

The 4th hexagram of the I Ching informed him, he was a rebellious youth, which didn't help.

Ju-Jumancy as practiced in the fetish district of Addis Ababa, was abhorrent to him, because of the tortures he remembered his step sisters inflicting on their porcelain dolls, so he gave it a miss.

He tried casting rice, or *Kau Uara*, but saw nothing in the patterns of grains that suggested numbers or letters.

Knissomancy, or divination by incense, made him sneeze, and so he didn't persist for long.

Lampadomancy, which was achieved by staring at flames, in this case a lighter held before his face, since candles weren't readily available, made his eyes water and burned his thumb, but that was all.

He would have liked to have a go at *Labiomancy*, but since no vaginas were available for consultation, he had to think of something else.

Machulomancy, or divination by the spots of skin, told him very little, even though he studied his entire body with the aid of a mirror, other than he had a large birthmark, like a knife pointing up his spine, just above the hairline of his buttocks. He found this most disturbing, not least for what it said about his relationship with Brünhilda, who he'd have thought would have commented on it, but then she never noticed anything, unless it was staring her in the face, and sometimes not even then.

Using a Ouija board, he attempted *Necyomancy,* but none of the damned souls he imagined he summoned, gave him more than 4 letter words in reply, which of course was far short of the 13 characters he was sure he needed.

Omphalomancy he guessed would take too long, since it involved studying one's navel for protracted periods, so he didn't bother, as time was pressing.

Next on his list was *Phyllomancy*, or divination by leaves, which seemed hopeful at first, but all the markings which he perceived on the leaves collected from the little balcony outside were runic in character, rather than relating to the alphabet, or numbers.

Quakomancy, or divining by earth tremors, wasn't possible, given that London is underpinned by deep deposits of clay, which absorbs all but major earth movements.

Rhapsodomancy, which required declaiming classical poetry, also didn't work, either because the poems he recited were too short, or they were by modern poets who deviated from traditional rhyming meters.

Scapulimancy, involving studying the markings of scapulae, he had always wanted to try, however no shoulder bones of Ox nor beast were to be had at the only butchers he managed to locate, operating out of surplus Mr Whippy van in Cunning Lane Market, which sold cheap pre-packaged cuts of meat, to queuing EastEnders who love a bargain.

While at the market, Wolfgang tried *Transataumancy*, but all he heard was babble from people in the crowded lane, and certainly nothing that would constitute a password thirteen characters long, which anyway he supposed might include numbers.

Not giving up on T, banging his head repeatedly against a wall he tried *Traumamancy*, but that only made him see stars, and the bumps on his forehead told him nothing, despite consulting a pamphlet on phrenology he'd found in a gutter by the second-hand book stalls in the market.

Umbormancy, or divination by shadows, proved next to useless, since all Saturday and most of Sunday the sky was overcast, which wouldn't have been that much of a problem, only when he squinted, he noticed an interference pattern, which seemed to be spread right across it. He wondered was that from the electronic signals from the black devices everyone seemed to have? Whatever the source, any shadows were too vague and fuzzy to obtain any positive result.

Videomancy, as relating to film, was a thought, but since he fancied none of the movies playing at nearby cinemas, he decided against.

Water witching, or dowsing he had already tried, dropping pebbles in a bucket staring at concentric circles, and so that was out.

Xylomancy gave him a splinter, after he rubbed the plank of wood he was studying the wrong way.

He spilled a lot of salt trying *Ydromancy*, but nothing came up, other than what he superstitiously tossed over his left shoulder.

Finally reaching Z, he would have tried *Zooomancy*, however the only animal available to observe, was himself, so as a last resort he decided to go back a few letters and try *Spermomancy*.

However, even divination by his golden oaties which had been a sure-fire method in the past, didn't work. For when, using his squinting technique, he stared into the glass vial into which he had just ejaculated, all he made out in the random placement of golden flecks in his semen, was the image of a knife, which was disturbingly like the birthmark on his backside. He didn't want to think about that, and decided take a nap instead, and so fell asleep with his head resting on the top of the imp laptop, a brand name he still didn't realise was an abbreviation of Imperitor, just as though the balcony windows a spectacular harvest moon, full and golden, rose over the rooftops across the street, bathing the crown of his head with ethereal lunar rays.

W hen Wolfgang awoke around 9am on Monday morning after falling asleep in the small hours with his head resting on the laptop, exhausted by all his attempts at divination over the weekend, it was with the image which was all he remembered from a dream of a heart crossed by two arrows, making an X. The arrow heads were inscribed with a S and a Z on opposite sides of the heart which was black and dripping – not with blood, his first thought, for the drops appeared to be brown and foamed where they fell.

That all has got to be to do with the password, was Wolfgang's first thought. Obviously, the S, indicated Skull, the X love and the Z, ZaZa. But then he reconsidered, for despite *skullloveszaza,* having 14 characters the result seemed too simple somehow. Besides, he reasoned, ZaZa would never acknowledge love for or from anyone. In her view, lust trumped all, which perhaps accounted for the heart being black instead of the usual red. Would Zaza, with her monstrous appetites, ever be satisfied with just one X? Obviously, no. Then there were the foaming drips in his dream to consider. Was that beer? He wondered, as he remembered the first time he laid eyes on Skull in the Tallyho bar in Snaresburgh, back in the Kingdom, grinning evilly behind empty bottles of his favourite brand of Australian lager beer, cluttering his table in the corner from under which he dispensed deals on Friday nights to the local yokels, who depended on him for their drugs.

Considering how much Skull drank of his favourite brand of beer, Wolfgang reasoned that he had to love 4X lager at least as much as he did Zaza, so he typed in, skullXXXXzaza, but then, reflecting that Inuit grandiosity was second nature to her, retyped her name in caps. Then, not giving himself time to change his mind, he stabbed his index finger on the enter key. A moment of panic, when the screen went blank, before an image of the Northern Lights unfurled across it, and he was in.

Her files were held in two separate locations. From his first look it seemed pretty obvious, that 'Diary of a Pussy Kat' were an ongoing account of her daily doings, whereas The WC directory opened onto the cartoonish interior of a log cabin. On the facing wall were 10 identical doors, all in a line. Above them was a flashing header, which warned that clicking on the wrong door, would detonate a micro bomb concealed in the laptop, and result in death or serious injury.

Fuck that for a laugh, Wolfgang muttered, deciding to leave well alone, but then, with a spasmodic twitch, the, he inadvertently clicked on the third door. That prompted the appearance of a second drop down sign, which flashed the words, *Bang Bang You're Dead*, as on the screen below, as toilet door No 3, swung open to reveal the icon of an igloo. Wolfgang suspected that there was no bomb, and clicking on any of the doors would have shown the same igloo icon, but even had he wanted to, there was no time to test his theory.

When a few minutes later, the 49e bus, pulled up at the stop outside, Wolfgang was successfully copying the last of ZaZa's private files onto a memory stick which somewhat uncharacteristically he'd had the forethought to buy at Cunning Lane Market the day before. It had been touch and go, and a couple of times he thought he'd pressed the wrong key and erased all the files, but somehow he managed to complete what seemed an excessively complicated operation, just as from downstairs, he heard her key in the lock, the front door opened, and her step sounded on the parquet floor of the hall below.

'You sure are looking perkier than when I left you on Friday, despite those dark circles under your eyes,' ZaZa said, as she settled into her seat behind her Louis XIV typing station. 'Been out clubbing?'

'No, just pleased to see you.' Wolfgang shrugged, grinning back at her from his sputnik chair. 'Did you get up to anything nice over the Weekend?'

'Yes actually, Skull charted a boat and the services of a handsome Spanish guitarist to serenade me, with money earned from his new landscape gardening business, and on Sunday we sailed up river from Tower Bridge to Thamesmead. The return journey sailing down river, was very romantic with Skull reciting his favourite Edward Lear poem to the sound of classical guitar music, as we watched the full moon rising over the softly flowing waters.'

'So glad to hear it.' Wolfgang said entirely insincerely, his guts spasming as usual whenever Skull's name came up.

'And what does your Lairdship have planned for this session?'

'I want to get back to the Melon.'

'I thought you'd given up trying to recreate that session.'

'Well I wouldn't have to if you'd made carbon copies on the old Imperitor typewriter back at the castle.

'Not that again,' ZaZa, sighed. 'Just be glad this is the digital age now. Why don't you to cut to the aftermath, where the meat is.'

'The Executioners Tale?'

'That's the one,' she nodded, 'I really like that story.'

'I thought offering advice was out with the terms of our R.A.S. contract?'

'It is, but the R.A.S. allows the occasional exception.'

'Maybe you could make an exception and go back to our old arrangement with the porridge.'

'No way,' she laughed, 'Now what's to be?

'Melon.'

'You seem adamant.'

'I am,' he growled, intensely irritated by her persistence. No, it was more than that, he thought, his irritation was *profound.*

'May I ask why? She said, smiling sweetly.

'That story I will save for later, meanwhile can we get back to Melon which if you recall is by the notable author Diogenes C. Horse.'

'As you like your lairdship, whenever you are ready,' Zaza said, her oversized fingers poised above the keys.

THE THIRTY NINE SPOTS

by Diogenes **C.** Horse.

I *was wrapped in black, my entire upper torso bandaged,
lying on a hospital bed, my skin burnt to a crisp, crackling
every time I winced. But worse that that, the pervading
smell of pork scratchings was making me hungry. How had all
this come about? I'd known the Mohican headbanger, herein
named Melon, in my youth, when I touted hash and acid, in the
pubs and Clubs of the Old town of Kingsburgh. At the time ...*

'Wolfgang?' ZaZa interrupted.

'What is it now!' A frustrated author thundered.

'I thought the title was supposed to be THE GLORY AND
THE ECSTASY?'

'I have decided to change it.'

'But shouldn't you consult Diogenes C. Horse first?'

'Don't be ridiculous, I am the author.' Dramatically, he
pointed to his chest, 'Now, where was I?'

'You were about to dictate Melon's back-story.'

'Was I?' Wolfgang grimaced, remembering when it all went
wrong, 'Oh yes, the Mohican Melon who thought he was Charles
Manson, and tried to take over the castle, after I generously

invited him up to do some blacksmith jobs, which was his trade. Fire and molten metal. Black magic, it turned out. I should have known, there were rumours. 'Well,' Wolfgang sat up, 'I sorted him out, true and proper. But I never got free of his curse, the black spot of Makumbe which would arrive on postcards, each a photo of the same voodoo skull, all 39 of them addressed to The Laird of Haggard with

scratchy black ink letters, like an inscription on a tombstone. Believe me. Gave me the shivers. Maybe they were from his son, who I saved from being sacrificed to Makumbe on the pyre Melon built in the yard, when I got the burns and the horrible smell which put me off pork scratchings for life?' Reflexively, he touched his cheek, 'This side of my face was totally barbecued, so bad you wouldn't have believed.'

'But there's no scarring? ZaZa interrupted, peering at him, owlishly.

'I always heal quickly,' he said, sanguine and for once not at all heated, 'but I had put all of my mind in order to concentrate on speeding up the healing process, so I wasn't at all surprised, when three days later, my bandages were removed, to hear the medical experts gathered at the bedside, all agree that I was a medical marvel,' he shrugged, modestly. 'But then instead of being released, as I expected to Brünhilda, who had been waiting patiently all this time in *my* Lamborghini, outside the entrance, a miracle in itself, being that she had other things to do, suddenly I was belted up in a gurney, and lifted into an ambulance, which drove very fast to a distant part of the hospital.

As the back doors opened, I spied roof spires, turrets, gargoyles and on the lower floors, barred windows.

Then I passed under the elaborate carved letters, embellishing a stone scroll above the entrance declaring, 'The Bethesda Institute for the Criminally Insane' which made me oddly pleased, for I had often wondered what Victorian lunatic asylums were like on the inside. The entrance hall however was not at all as I had anticipated from the building's gothic exterior. Instead of statues of pedagogue and benefactors set in niches, tall stained glass windows filtering rays of soft light onto marble floors, and moral exhortations in gold leaf around the walls, as I expected, everything was blindingly white: the uniforms of the staff, the tiles on the partition walls, the desk at Admissions, even the lino - all of it was harshly lit by fluorescent strip lights, recessed in a false ceiling, instead of soaring into groined vaults, as I imagined it doing behind white polystyrene panels, claustrophobically close above.

Lying on the gurney, listening to the hubbub around me, I learned that I was detained under a Section 22 Order, which is only ever invoked *when the ball goes up*. Then, while I had the sides of my head shaved by an unseen barber, who grabbed my head from behind, I suspected, in preparation for electro-convulsive therapy, phone calls were made, seeking clearer instructions with what to do with me. Faces appeared above me, examined me from behind medical lenses, as fingers poked my limbs, testing reactions. When it was judged I offered no more resistance, I was unstrapped from the gurney, allowed to sit up, given three brightly coloured capsules, which I palmed, and only pretended to swallow. A mere bystander, while discussions of my case continued, my pleas to visit the toilet were ignored, until, it seemed that my registration was finally in order, when the manager who had been on the phone all this time, announced I was ready for processing, and directed two guards, one male and the other female, though it was hard to tell them apart, to escort me upstairs, for my induction. But then when I protested once more that my bladder was bursting, the manager grudgingly allowed a toilet call on the way.

As with the entrance hall, three floors below, the room was white tiled and harshly lit by fluorescent tubes. All was blinding white except for a rusted catch securing the fan light of a window, high above the handbasins. Just as I spotted the anomalous catch, a knock from the female guard on the other side of the toilet door, drew my male minder away. Taking advantage of his temporary absence, clambering onto a sink, and stretching my full height I popped the window catch with a sharp blow from my elbow. But then, in my haste to exit the window before the guard reappeared, pushing out the frame I was pitched head first down a valley of the roof between two spires, my slide only prevented from continuing into the shadowed depths of an inner courtyard by an accumulation of debris from the previous winter's gales, choking the gutter behind a gargoyle rain spout. When alarms sounded somewhere in the building below, I hardly noticed, concentrating on negotiating a skirt of slippery slates extending above the eves, towards a metal ladder which accessed a lower flat roof. At the end of it was a low parapet topped by spikes, and beyond that an old oak tree, with spreading branches, close to the building. Calculating I could leap across to it and then climb down the tree trunk, I took a running jump over the spikes, but missed my target branch, and instead landed hard on my arse on soft earth, ten feet below, my fall fortunately broken by rose bushes.

Bursting from the rose bushes, bandages unravelling like an Egyptian mummy resurrected from Ancient Thebes, I hailed a little bus which appeared on a joke road that cut through the trimmed lawns of the hospital grounds. Driven by a bright-eyed OAP with a pencil moustache, and a winged badge on his lapel of his blue serge uniform which read 'Eddie.'

I supposed the bus was to transport patients around the hospital. However rather than picking any of the people standing at the bus stop before the next roundabout, Eddie slung a sharp left. The little bus reminding me of a champagne cork, as we popped out of a side entrance onto the main road. No one else on board, just me and Eddie grinning like this was WWII again, and we were on special ops mission – that was the sense I had watching him head down over the steering wheel, overtaking traffic all the way along the busy three-lane road into the city. A few minutes later we arrived safely at the bus station, at the stance reserved for the ancillary hospital bus service, operated by ex-Royal Airforce servicemen, which Eddie pointed out, before shaking my hand as I thanked him for his sudden providential appearance, and fast service.

'Anyway, the point is, when I got back Brünhilda blamed me for it all, even though the episode with Melon, had only lasted a week, three days of which anyway were in out-of-the-way pubs across the Kingdom, where I hoped I wouldn't be recognised. Without success trying to drown him in whisky, pulling him out of fights with coalminers, telling angry people he wasn't the US all-time supreme pool champion as he had claimed, denying I was a Mohican brother, despite the shaved sides of my head, spending a fortune buying drinks to placate everyone he insulted. Getting them drunk, but not Melon. Before someone gave me a card with the number of a confidential private ambulance service, which is how I finally got rid of him. Never so glad as when watching the ambulance speeding away, sirens howling, taking Melon to the hospital and the same secure facility I had recently departed, his face so bashed up, he was unrecognisable as anything else but a Melon. My wallet in his pocket, and watch on his wrist which Brünhilda inscribed to me one birthday. A sacrifice I was only too willing to make, in the circumstances, despite the loss it represented ...' He panted, his face red with emotion.

'Wolfgang, in my experience, authors begin at the beginning and not the end,' she laughed. 'Or maybe reversing the normal process is just a dyslexic thing.'

'No **just** about it,' Wolfgang snarled, 'The beginning of this story was the end. The end of the good times at the Castle,' sadly he shook his head, 'things were never the same with Brünhilda, I wish I'd never met him.'

'I am sure you do. Perhaps you should take a break, smoke a spliff and compose yourself.'

'I thought your professional association barred you from offering advice to your employers.' Wolfgang glowered.

'I was speaking ...' she hesitated uncharacteristically, 'If you must know, as a friend.' She said, her jaw clenched, as though she had to force the words out.

'A friend, am I?' Wolfgang made a fist, 'With friends like you who needs enemies?'

'As you like it.' She said coldly.

'Oh god, I am sorry,' Wolfgang blurted, slumping in his chair, 'It has just come to me. ZaZa, I've lost everything, the Castle, my marriage, the glory days, all of it, I'll never get it back.'

'So, is this the end for the Laird?'

'No,' Wolfgang snapped out of his slump, 'they'll never take that away from me.'

'And the book?'

'Don't worry, you're still employed,' he glared. 'We've just got to the end of the beginning, that's all. I'll make this volume about something else.' His eyes narrowed, 'Yea, this new branded world I'm having to come to terms with, that's what.'

'So, do you have a story to begin with?'

'Yes, I do, as it happens.'

ZARGON, *the* **WICKED SORCERER**

of the **NORTH**

by **Fanshaw Ramsbottom-Quartz**

CHAPTER 1

*A*fter receiving another report of a Slave Revolt, this time from far-flung Sector Z, where the Inuit Empire of the North butted up against the equatorial wall girdling the world, Zargon decided to pay a long overdue visit to the Great Ice Hall at the North Pole where the umbilical cords of his subjects were stored from when they were taken at birth and held until death, in sub-zero temperatures. No one knew better than him of the vital intelligence the umbilicals provided with every twitch and flip, in their irradiated copper bottomed containers, relating to their subjects' present activities and future intentions – information that up till a few days before, at least on the face of it, had been unfailingly reliable, but no longer, given the coordinated revolts in the adjoining provinces of X and Y, which the latest evidence suggested had been long in the planning. That was more than worrying, for it implied that the data from smaller, but even more important House of the Placenta where the cauls of the 'chosen' elite of the Empire, including his own, were stored, had also been compromised.

The monitoring system he devised had been a considerable improvement on the previous method of surveillance employed by the Nonchucks, as the security police were known. That system had been based on nail pairings and hair clippings – which can score as high as unbillicals, but only in controlled conditions, when kept at absolute zero, which of course is hard to maintain over long periods, even in an Inuit Ice house.

Situated precisely on the geographical point that is the North Pole, the Ice Hall, as its name suggests, was large, however despite its enormous size it was rather less of a hall than an igloo, being built in the classic Inuit form, from huge shaped blocks of ice put together in a giant dome.

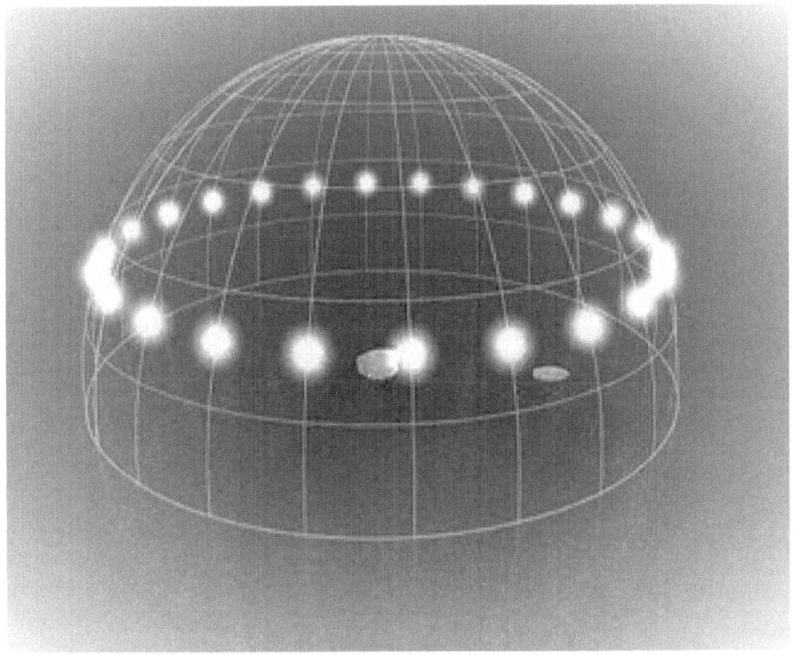

Inside, the soaring dome was suffused with a blue glow from electrical fields, illuminating the racked umbilicals, bobbing in bubbling blue fluid, in their copper-bottomed bell jars. Monitors above, recording every movement of the umbilicals, relayed the data, to terminals at the end of the long tiers which divided the space into long rows, above which were suspended, alphabetical letters, designating in which sector, the umblicals subjects had been born. Everything was apparently as it should be, no red warning lights winking on any of the monitors, to disturb the even blue glow suffusing everything under the giant dome. And that was the issue which should have been picked up by the soon to be deceased caul formerly in charge of the Ice Hall, for there never had been a time when a significant proportion of his slave subjects did not harbour ill thoughts and evil intentions against their caul overlords, and their Magus.

*By rights, with half the population in sectors X, Y and now with Z too involved in some way, the same proportion of arrays, should have been flashing multiple warning lights, but none were evident as he paced between the rows, under the soaring blue dome. Obviously, Zargon thought, to catch the deviant thoughts of umbilicals **and** cauls, they needed to devise a total surveillance system...*

'That's your Session over!' ZaZa suddenly announced.

'It's not that time already, surely?' Wolfgang protested.

'Yep!' ZaZa said happily, slipping a memory stick containing her files into a pocket of her brief case. She pointed an oversized finger at the screen, 'Look, all you have to do is enter your new password, in the box here. I've written it on this,' she said, placing a card on the desk. ' She stood up, impatient to go. 'I'll see you in a couple of days, at the same time.'

'Why not tomorrow?' Wolfgang asked.

'Something's come up, I can't get out of,' she shrugged. 'Don't worry I'll make up for the lost hours later,' she added vaguely, before declaring, 'And for once I am looking forwards to the next part and learning more about the ancient Inuit empire!'

'Can't you spare a minute? I need you to point out things I should know about the laptop.'

'Nope,' she said, reaching for the door, 'I have my bus to catch. Byeeee!'

Despite his protestations, Wolfgang was glad to see her go. Watching from the french windows, he waited until the 49e bus pulled up at the stop outside. Only when it drove off with the baggage safely on board, did he turn around, an expression of unholy glee on his face.

He was about to sit down before the laptop open on the Louis XIV table, when a noise in the house from somewhere below drew his attention.

Before going downstairs to investigate the noises coming from the basement, reaching on the half landing Wolfgang stepped into the kitchen, and took a chopping knife from the cutlery drawer, but then, catching sight of his reflection in the chrome of the overengineered Russian kitchen units, he hesitated, feeling the knife in his hand as a live thing ... Perhaps it was better if he went unarmed, he reconsidered, carefully replacing the large knife-, which momentarily had seemed to have mutated into a sinuous snaking blade, before resuming its shape as he firmly closed the drawer. He didn't want to be had up for GBH, or worse, murder. Who knows what an investigation into his past might turn-up? And anyway, he reasoned, it might just be a rat in one of the locked basement cupboards.

No rat, as it turned out, instead, as Wolfgang threw open the door to the basement, who should step out of one of the cupboards carrying a black suitcase, but Plain John.

'What the fuck?' Wolfgang blurted.

'Hi mate,' Plain John looked round, guiltily. 'Just pickin' up sum 'fings.' He said, shutting the cupboard door, which locked automatically behind him.

'What's in that mate?' Wolfgang pointed at the bulky suitcase.

'Personal mate, personal,' Plain John grinned, setting the heavy case down on the concrete floor and flexing his hand, 'Yew know 'ow it is.' Then, when Wolfgang's belligerent expression didn't change, he tapped his nose, 'Trust me mate, yew down't want ta know.'

Wolfgang laughed, 'So that's the way it is.'

'Ac'ually mate I ownly come foah it, 'cos we're gowin' to 'ave to cleah this ploice owt.'

'Really,' Wolfgang's eyes narrowed, 'Why?'

'The big boss just got send down foah 10 yeahs in Moscow, and the Mad Monk is toikin' ovah.'

'So, he's some sort of religious zealot?' Wolfgang said, imagining a Rasputin figure, with a long straggly beard and mesmeric eyes.

Plain John looked blank, then shook his head, 'Na, that's just 'is nickname. He's a roight cunt, believe me, a roight cunt.'

'So, what's that to me?'

'He wants awl the propertaes put up foah sale, soon as, mate, soon as.'

'Oh, that's great news,' Wolfgang scowled, 'And just when I was getting settled in.'

'Ow, down't worry mate, there's a dose of 'owses in the West End to gow oan the market first. But Oi'll need to cleah-out the furniture upstairs.'

'Couldn't I do that?'

'That'd 'elp mate, that'd 'elp.' Plain John said, reaching towards the switch on the wall that operated the garage door. 'It's awll gowin' to get dumped anywoi.'

*

ROACH here again...

25 Enero, 2028.

Room 407, Hotel Belvoir,Placa del Armas, Punto Arenas. *Overlooking the UPS Office which is closed, like the airport and most anything else here because of the General Strike. Meaning I am trapped in El Nueva Republico de Patagonia, until the strike ends, which doesn't look like it will happen anytime soon, given the evident anger of the population against the .1% Junta, their new rulers.*

I have a confession to make, the typescripts of sessions 17-43 which included the Executioner's tale, were forever lost through my impetuosity, which sometimes knows no bounds.

Wolfgang never knew, and I never volunteered the information, fearing his wrath, being as I am a cowardly cockroach. It's an easy admission to make now that he is not around. In my defence, it is an observable fact that cockroaches are cowardly by nature, scurrying to the nearest crack in the wall, at the merest hint of a threat. However, it was a mean thing to do, throwing his precious typescripts into a fire, and watching the pages blacken, twist and curl in the flames, all those irreplaceable words of his errant genius lost, going up in smoke. But I was angry with him, years of resentment over the way he took me for granted, while lavishing his attention on the latest visitor to the castle. Never more than when the pale Inuit woman with the huge hands that looked like they belonged to a murderer, turned up at the Castle's North gate, seeking employment. At night, tucked away in my burrow I would dream those giant hands were scuttling like crabs about on the ground above my head, blindly searching for the way into my burrow. Was that guilt over what I had done, or was it my fear of them which prompted me to commit the crime against my master – which came first I really don't know? But then, the brain capacity of Cockroaches is small, and our memories unreliable.

After the irritating interruption in the basement, Wolfgang got back to the main business in hand —namely investigating Zaza's files, which he'd had the forethought to copy before she deleted them from the laptop, at the end of their last session.

DIARY *OF A* PUSSY KAT

*(**ZaZa**'s notes in the field)*

23 Wenativitu Piu.

Wolf hid something when I arrived for work this morning. Before I could grab the unusual looking device off the table, he whipped it away, grinning hugely as he stuffed it into a pocket of his moth-eaten tartan dressing gown. All thru the session its bulge continued to irritate me, as he paced around the room, declaiming, between lolling in his chair, fishing for suggestions, swivelling annoyingly and rolling larger than usual joints. About the size of a paperback book, the device had a rectangular viewing screen, in which dots of colour seemed to move.

Appearances are deceptive. Wolfgang reacts lightning fast when he needs to. With his languid air, and slow speech, he pretends to be a bumptious fool, but is anything but.

Despite the fog he spreads about wherever he goes, behind his thick eyelashes to make the girls jealous, and the hash he habitually smokes, his eyes are always searching. A most interesting case. So many secrets.

25 Waniveutu Wi.

Frustratingly, again the tests have come back inconclusive. H or L? we still don't know. Descendent of the original Fenhir back in the day or just a freak of nature, that is the QSTN. Ha! It would seem I am assigned, a while yet. But what I most want to know is why slippers? And does he even suspect? It seems not.

26 Wenativitu Piu.

He will keep shying away from the Executioner's Tale, which was among the papers burnt by that miserable cockroach infesting Haggard, who hid in a burrow I could never find. Fortunately for Inuits the verminous creatures cannot survive long above the Arctic Circle, it being too cold for their pathetic constitutions. Of course, we have the notes I took back at the Castle, but we need the Executioner's Tale, if only for the detail it provides about the Makumbe Ritual and Melon's metal working talents with the Black Dog meteorite, otherwise we'll never put the whole picture together. Though the initial tests at the hospital were disappointingly inconclusive, the materialization of Fenhir's black dog in the 22nd session was telling, at the time convincing good old WC we must go on. Then, only last week, a knife turned up at an auction in the Kingdom, which we think is the one. Forensic analysis confirmed that the thumb and palm prints on the blade had been impressed into the metal when it was still molten. And what do you know? The prints were verified as belonging to Iain Cuthbert Hamilton, aka Melon aka Grand Wizard of the High Synod of Makumbe, presently assumed to be in the Caribbean. However, the very fact his prints are indelibly marked on the blade gives credence to Wolfgang's claim made in session 24 that Melon forged the knife when in a trance state, with his fingers twisting and drawing out the molten metals into its final serpentine form – the prescribed length from the shoulder clavicle to the heart, as the ritual requires. But then, in session 25, Melon goes too far, and Wolfgang has to rescue Melon's insensible young son, about to be sacrificed to the Voodoo god. In the role of the hero, he steps into the fire lighted around the base, pushes past Melon, up to his knees in flames mumbling incantations, grabs the still red hot blade from his hands, and clambers up the flaming pyre where the boy is staked, wrapped in a wet sheet which is starting to smoulder, and cuts him free - thereby sustaining his third degree burns, from which he recovered so quickly, which of course which led to the inconclusive tests at the hospital. Trouble is, as my old wing commander said, in my last debriefing, no two versions are sufficiently close to signify this laird is anything but a dyed in the butt hole genuine lycomorph - which when I thought of it, could mean either or, which is typical of WC - and reason enough to stay on the case despite the expenses, I continue to rack up with my daily commute on the 49e. Ha ha.

1 Kenatenpegi Piu

Today being first day of the month of Kenatenpegi Piu, following the full moon of Wenativitu Piu, when the ancestor spirit Rutting Caribou descends on Inuit couples in igloos, and leads them in lewd acts, and grotesque displays, which are considered a gift of power for the coming season, indicating the hunting will be good when the sea freezes over and the tusk of the Ancestor Walrus and the Spear of Herman the Hunter rise in the night sky. Lest I forget, lest I forget.

(The following entry, seems to mark a significant point on the trajectory of my journey, but what exactly I don't know. I must think on it.)

Skull is a Dutch baboon who only believes in his prick, despite his claims of alien encounters at cross roads, and demonic seductions in his jokey tales. After last night's performance with the trumpet, as we sailed under Tower Bridge, exposing himself to ogling tourists cramming the sides of passing cruise boats all the way to Greenwich, I have decided I don't really know him anymore, and wonder if I ever did at all. Sure, Skull was always borderline, which is part of the reason the alt-CIA recruited him, but in the field we are supposed to stay below the radar, which he wasn't doing prancing with about the deck waving his perpetually hard knob, necking champagne, playing the lupine baboon, howling at the full moon rising over the river. Then, on the way back that Spanish guitarist, who turned out to be a Greek, got into the spirit and pressed his attention on Skull. But after a few minutes, becoming bored with his clumsy humping and girly giggles, Skull heaved him over the handrail, and stood pissing on the guitarist's head, as I hauled him out of the water, on the lifebelt I threw him. Zoth knows, though unable to stop laughing, inwardly I was seething, intent on blood. When we *got back, I endured the inevitable priapic assault, during which predictably he fell asleep. But then this morning, I had to laugh at the little boy lost look on his face, his plaintive pleas of moon madness, on his knees begging forgiveness from his Empress. Still, I wonder if his munificence hiring the boat and his werewolf dance on the deck were misdirection, and he has finally gone rogue, as WC always predicted. I can only conclude that with recent developments what was a possibility has become a distinct probability, considering the thickness of the wad in his pocket, the £50's he dispenses like recycled condoms to a convention of Dutch sex workers in Azerbaijan, where they have none, from his new business which hardly ticks over, with the three gardeners he pays, playing dominos all day in their miserable hut he calls his office, which when I think about is the duplicate of the yacht club hut he hid out in all those months watching the castle - typical of his sentimental choices, curse him. The landscape gardening business is supposed to be a cover, clearly though, he is laundering money from somewhere. I shall have to watch him more closely. Meanwhile, at the other end of my 49e bus daily commute, my 'employer' continues to pose unsettling questions.*

There was only one record in the Igloo file behind the third door in the log cabin page.

It read:

Something's come up. Meet me, 23ʳᵈ, usual room, 3pm, Boreal Tower. Disgraced 'hairy' Marjory's been replaced at Reception, so remember Wednesday's password is **Base Values***. Old Walrus Tusk says be on time, or miss the action. W.C.*

*

Wolfgang didn't know if he should be angry, amused or just plain mad after reading the first file of ZaZa's daily doings. Why was she having his porridge tested? Was it to be the secret ingredient in some vastly expensive anti-wrinkle crème? Furthermore, what did Zaza mean with her aside about slippers? And who was this WC with the walrus Tusk who ZaZa was to report to in the Boreal Tower? Could he be CIA, meaning the Central Inuit Agency, was nosing into his affairs? If so, why? The answer seemed obvious, when he thought about it. Weapons grade space glass, the same as orbited the world's polar regions in giant mirrors without which his schematic device wouldn't work, if indeed it did at all. That being something of a sore point, as lately he had begun to wonder if he had imagined its efficacy and whether the few positive results were mere coincidence. Was his whole world falling apart, or just the fantasy construction he had put on it? Should he see that as a welcome development or was it bad? He really didn't know what to think. Add that to Plain John's unwelcome news, delivered an hour before, that his tenure as a caretaker, was soon to end, together with Jaw's failure to respond to his latest messages, and Zaza needing paid at the end of the week, suddenly it felt like the walls were pressing in. Worse still he had run out of dope, and no longer had any contacts in London, meaning he would have to take the Tube to Brixton, and hang about likely street corners in the hope of being approached by a Rasta dealing second grade weed, rather than the primo hash he was used to. Of course, he could pull in a favour with ZaZa, and get her to ask Skull to use his connections, but that was a route best not travelled, since there was no knowing where it would end. In a ditch he imagined, either him or Skull bleeding out, given the abyssal depths of their mutual animosity. Best to leave well alone. But wasn't he missing something he suspected was hidden in plain sight, or as near as damnit?

Lying on his side, on the basement's concrete floor, squinting at the small mirror he'd taped to the pole and pushed under the cupboard door, Wolfgang let out a low whistle. He'd wanted a smoke to clear his head and get his priorities straightened out, but surely what he beheld behind the door was excessive even by his standards ... If he wasn't mistaken, the back wall of the cupboard was stacked with kilo bars of black hash, individually wrapped in clingfilm – hence the absence of smell. There had to be at least 40 or 50 bars in the cupboard, he estimated, dyslexically losing count at the second attempt and getting a crick in the neck in the process. Surely plain John wouldn't miss just one, which would be more than ample for his present needs. But he couldn't exactly call out a locksmith, who he had heard are vetted by the police. So how to get past the cupboard's lock? Of course he could just bust in the door, and then skedaddle with the dope, which seemed the logical move, given that his tenure in the house was now sharply truncated, and sell it back in the Kingdom, far from the reach of East End gangsters, Russian oligarchs and their Systema thugs, thereby solving his money troubles at a stroke. But to do so would be unworthy of a Laird, even though presently only a lowly caretaker. He had given his word, and was honour bound. However, he needed that fucking smoke ...

'The garage door can't have closed properly, when you left. How else could they have got in?'

'Nothin's secure these days, trust me.' John said sadly, as he and Wolfgang stood surveying the damage to the cupboard door, 'Oi recon I must 'ave been followed heah, mate.'

'Lucky I heard them.'

'Lucky *thoi* run off, yew mean mate.'

'Knowing it wasn't you, coming down the stairs I made as much noise as possible, yelling blue murder, hoping they'd think there was more than just one of me.'

'Didn't catch na soight of them, mate?'

Wolfgang shook his head. 'When I got here the door was hanging off its hinges. Discretion being the better part of valour, I decided not to go outside, after them.'

'That were woise mate, woise.' Plain John nodded sagely, 'Villains in these parts pack them new Boreal semi-automatics as standard, an' ain't shy to use 'em. Not loike the owld d'ys when thoi 'ad mannahs and awsked questions befoah blastin' oaff. But this is the East End mate.' He shrugged - as if to say what did he expect. 'The East End!'

'I take it none are missing?' Wolfgang pointed at the bars of hash arranged on the concrete floor.

'Na,' Plain John shook his head, 'awl fifty's theah. I guess I owe yew wun, mate.'

'One would do,' Wolfgang grinned, picking up a brick.

'Na, couldn't spare that much, it's awl accounted foam. Theah's na slack with them Systema fuckers, mate, na slack at awl.' He paused, "s'ppose Oi could skim an ounce, would that do mate?'

His expectations of a kilo dashed, but happy to have something half decent to smoke to last him past the weekend, Wolfgang helped Plain John load the hash briquettes in the boot of the Alpha Romeo backed into the Garage before he drove off into the night, waving a gloved hand out of his window.

SESSION #3

ZaZa looked round in astonishment, as she entered the room, 'Where's all the furniture?' she said, looking around for a place to dump her coat.

'I kept the Louis XIV, the sputnik chair and the Kyrgyzstan rug as you can see.' Wolfgang said, reflexively patting his pocket, and the fat wad of notes he had received in exchange.

'But I need something to sit on.' She protested.

'There's a stool underneath the desk,' he extended a hand, 'Look, I've kept this hanger 'specially for your coat, and if you notice behind you there's still a hook on the back of the door.'

'I can hang it up myself, thank you,' she glowered, 'What did you do with it all?'

'The furniture?'

'What else do you think I mean?' She snarled, while prodding the cushioned seat of the stool with outsize fingers.

'I sold it all to a dealer specializing in Eastern European furniture, who I contacted via the SuperInk.'

'So, you are up to speed now.'

'I wouldn't claim that.' Wolfgang shrugged modestly, 'But I have an Inkpot message account now and I've got to say those Imp tutorials are excellent. I had a great couple of days working through them.'

'Stoned, I bet.'

'Absolutely. I got lucky and scored a nice bit, if you want to try some.'

'You know hash's not my bag, but I wouldn't say no to some speed.'

'Sorry, can't help you there,' Wolfgang shrugged, being not sorry at all, 'What's up?'

She sighed, 'I've had a very trying couple of days.'

'Skull been up to his tricks again?' Wolfgang asked, sitting back down on his sputnik chair.

'No,' she shook her head. 'For once it wasn't him.'

'What was going on then?'

'Can't say.'

'You mean won't. I never knew anyone who kept things so close to her, um, bosom,' he laughed, eyeballing what he regarded as her best feature.

'Wolfgang stop fishing. I like to keep the different parts of my life separate. And if I told you, it would only end up in one of your stories. Now are going to stop this crass repartee and start dictating?'

THE SANDS OF UHURU

by Siegfried Amundsen-Crampon

*U*sing his immensely powerful paws the Wolf Fenhir levelled the mountain ranges of the Southern continent of Uhurhu, and with his diamond claws scraped its plains down to the bedrock. As he scrabbled with his paws, the spoil piled up behind him in a stupendous embankment girdling the World. His furnace breath which had rendered its vertiginous sides sheer and smooth as glass also boiled off the seas, lakes and rivers, which, evaporating as steam, formed towering clouds extending into the upper troposphere. These drifted to the far north, and fell as snow as the dense cloud cover cooled the top half of the planet. For decades the blizzards continued unabated, thereby increasing the weight and depth of the ice cap. A process that continued *long after spread of ice was halted by the barrier of Great wall. All this had resulted from Fenhir's actions.*

However, whether by oversight or not, the great Wolf had neglected to perform his last task set him by the great sorcerer, who had freed him from imprisonment in the Upperworld. This was to cauterise the underground cities where the its serfs had lived, when not labouring for the Ultimos, the .1% of the .1% who in Anthropocene times had divided the entire land surface of theGreat Southern Continent of Uhurhu between themselves, living in sybaritic luxury, in vast rolling estates they called Demesnes – borrowing the word from a long dead language of an ancient empire, whose patricians, like the Ultimos, had enslaved a world.

'That's all I can manage today.' Wolfgang panted, tearing off his shirt, buttons flying as he dropped it on the floor. 'This session's over.' He announced, rubbing his neck which like the rest of him glistened with sweat, while standing staring at the back of his other hand.

'You can't stop now.' she protested. 'That was your best yet.'

'I don't care,' Wolfgang grunted.

'Take a break, smoke a spliff, and then get back to it. You still have two hours left.'

'No, no, I can't deal with that story. Seriously, it's too much,' he said, sitting back down, clasping a hand to his clammy forehead.

'Why?' she demanded, standing staring down at him slumped in his sputnik chair.

He looked up, 'Roll me a spliff, please. I don't think I could manage.' He pointed, 'all the stuff's on the tray there, on the floor.

'Wolfgang you are hysterical.' She said, back behind her desk, clumsily sticking cigarette papers together with her outsize fingers.

'No, no, it's that story.' He shook his head, as if to clear it from his mind.

'You must explain. I need to understand why you are behaving like this.' She insisted.

'It ... it's ... W...' he spluttered.

'Wolfgang calm yourself, take a deep breath, and talk slowly.'

'Ok, yea, yea.' He breathed, staring at his trembling hands, 'you're right. I need to understand this too.'

'Damn right, I've never seen you act this way.' She said, sounding genuinely concerned.

'ZaZa, it's this wolf Fenhir. As I was dictating, I felt my throat thickening, my chest swelling, my hands becoming monstrous paws, great flames issuing my mouth, it was so ... so real, I almost can't believe I am me, with normal fingernails instead of enormous claws made of fucking diamonds, a hound of hell bigger than a fucking mountain range...'

'You are going to have to come back to this story,' ZaZa said, passing him a badly rolled spliff, and holding out a lighter.'

'Am I fuck!' Wolfgang said, lighting the spliff.

'Don't you realise Wolfie, you've hit pay dirt, this is tremendous. A totally different level from the other stories.'

'I don't care. I'd kill myself first.' He said, just as a heavy knock, sounded from the front door below.

Who the fuck?' Wolfgang jerked up in his chair, as more knocks thundered, all thoughts of Fenhir forgotten. 'ZaZa go look who's there, please. No one knows I'm here. But be careful you're not seen.'

'It's two big men,' she reported back from by the French windows. 'and there's what looks like a furniture van, parked on the bus stop. From their facial tattoos, I think the pair are Russian.'

'Oh god,' Wolfgang groaned, 'Quick, before they see you, come back from the window and hand me your ...' he snapped his fingers, forgetting the word, 'Your call thingie without a chord.'

'My what?' she said.

'Your phone pocket device thing.'

'Oh, you mean my foby.'

'Yea, yea, that's it. Quick, I need to call someone.'

'Do you know these men?' she said, passing him her foby.

'No, but you're right, they're Russians I'm sure,' he reverted to a hoarse whisper as downstairs the banging resumed on the front door. 'How do you work this thing?' he said staring at the device's screen, which was showing the number he had just entered.

'Press that button at the bottom on the right,' she pointed an oversize finger, 'that's right. Now, is it ringing?'

'Yea, yea,' Wolfgang said, pressing it to his ear, covering the foby with his other hand to shut out the loud banging from downstairs.

There was a click, then the ringing stopped, followed by a silence. After a moment a gruff voice said, 'Who is this?'

'John is that you?' Wolfgang said urgently.

'Yea?'

'John, it's me, The caretaker.'

'I thought Oi told yew to cawll from a fackin' phone box. Wot is it mate? Oi'm busy.'

'John, right now there's two Russian looking heavies outside banging on the front door.'

'Ow, thoi were quick. Ow. Ow. I meant to foby you about that, mate. Except I forgot yew down't 'ave wun.'

'Phone me about what?' Wolfgang said, a dreadful suspicion forming in his mind.

'They're to pick up the furniture mate.'

'But you told me to dump it.'

'Yea, yea,' Plain John muttered vaguely, 'That's awl chynged since the new boss arrived. 'E luvs that retro sputnik shit, an' wants it for 'is pent'ouse we're fitting out in the new tower.'

'Well, they can't have it right now.'

'Whoi mate? Whoi?'John sounded alarmed

'I got rid of it all, *as you suggested John.*'

'Well you'd better get it back, *and sharpish*, otherwise you and me,' John's voice raised a pitch, as downstairs the knocking suddenly ceased. 'Are dead goners mate. Dead gonners!'

'Alright, John,' Wolfgang gulped, 'how long do we have?'

'I recon I can 'owld 'em orf a couple of days, but na more, mate. Na more. Moike suah you get it awl.'

'I will, John. I will. Just make sure you call those dogs off.'

'Oi'll do that roight now mate. Good luck mate. Good luck.'

Wolfgang was having doubts about his 4d map reader, which didn't seem to work in this new branded reality, something he suspected might be to do with the interference pattern across the sky, which at night seemed to shut-out the emanations of the stars, visible or not. He'd put so much dogged perseverance into the project, just like he had with the renovation of the castle, and look where that had got him, he reflected, exile and divorce –

Unless of course, Jaws succeeded in spinning out the court proceedings until doomsday, when he would have to forfeit his title, as all lairds must do, when they finally expire. Wolfgang wondered how soon that might be, given recent developments which should have showed up on the 4D map reader as a confluence of black of green lines, converging on his present location from distant points across the city. Instead there was a singular absence of activity in the neighbourhood. For all he knew those few instances when in the past the device seemed to work, was down to the random derangement of the universe – how the cards fell out, when the music stopped. Anything else was the projection of his deluded imaginings. Was there ever such a foolish Laird in the annals of the Kingdom he wondered?

With a sigh his thoughts turned to Brünhilda of the sulks, and his nights in the kitchen of the big house, measuring lines on the maps, which he should have spent in bed with her. Did his neglect set her on the course from adultery with Mickey - a hired hand with a reputation among the ladies of Snaresburgh as a cocksman, which he supposed Brünhilda felt obliged to test to prove her credentials as a lady, if for no other reason, than to discover if she actually existed. How could the rheumy reflection confronting her every morning from her dressing table mirror look so sad, when she was as happy as could be, wasn't she? Or so from his perspective of distance and time, he imagined her in her lonely turret dressing room.

Whereas meanwhile, some nine hundred miles to the south in London, he was regretting what he could no longer deny, and propositions which wouldn't holdup any more, those having expired on the journey to where he was now.

Trouble was, he was completely disinterested in whatever was brewing over his disposal of the Sputnik furniture. Yes, that about described his state of mind. In a word he was abstracted. But removed to where exactly? In a pocket of depression between the shifting lines which had been notable by their absence recently on the screen. No way around it, the device was a dud.

With his projects he was no different from his brainstorm father, and *his* projects. Horrible thought, but non the less pertinent. Like his déjà vu when he picked up what he'd thought was a dead moth from the back of a drawer in his studio, and

felt a tiny heart flutter between his fingers, as he remembered the moth costume Brünhilda had worn to a fancy-dress balls, which also had eyes on the wings she loved to spread. There and then, he resolved to drop the role of brusque brute he'd had to play, to keep the renovation of the castle on track, and in the future, to pay her more attention.

However, all too soon he forgot his laudable good intentions, and before long what had been a divergence of paths, became a permanent split. His fault, this time because he ploughed on with the second prototype, and took advantage of the poor Trappist technicians, who submitted to all his demands without a protest, only too happy it seemed, to work on something not involving death rays, miniaturising the little device's component parts at the space glass factory down in the Special Economic Zone, he reflected guiltily. A sudden spasm in his gut, reminding him of his paranoia he always felt slowing the car approaching the R.U. checkpoints at the end of the Scappa Flo bridge. In his lap a clear plastic wallet, containing the hand crafted passes and authorisations, that could have gotten him 4 years in the Rig B, the Kingdom's notorious jail on an artificial island, 200 miles out to sea, built from redundant oil rigs after the fossil fuel boom was over, where they sent serial killers, child molesters, subversives and dyslexic forgers like himself. But then he reasoned, in that case Brünhilda would at last have something to do, and be so taken up with the romance of making the round sea trip to the jail at least once a week – knowing her, cadging a ride in a helicopter, having tea with the prison Governor, being charmed by hoodlums, and flirting with the guards - divorce the last thing on her mind.

So instead of tragic hero, if he ever wants to play the returning one, he will have find a peace offering of sufficient munificence - a Muzo emerald of unequalled clarity, colour and fire, at least the size of a duck egg, to placate her wrath – or if that wasn't possible, a platinum tiara studded with 10 carat diamonds, and a full codpiece, the result of muscle exercises with tantric masters, and a regime of cold baths in preparation for ... doomsday, when he returned. If he ever got so lucky...

SESSION #4

Slumped in his chair Wolfgang woke with a start, and opened one eye, tentatively. No wonder he was cold, the french windows were half open, and one of the panes was broken, shards of glass scattered on the floor below. A branch blown down from one of the trees outside, high winds in the night he supposed. What time was it? From the sound of the traffic outside, and the low angle of the late autumn sun, slanting in the room, he guessed getting on for 10 am. God he was stiff. Zaza was due in half an hour, the room was a mess and he was still in his McNemo tartan dressing gown. Really, he should get dressed and tidy up before the 49e bus delivered the baggage to the stop below, but he was so weary, his limbs leaden, and his eyelids just about as heavy. Bad dreams he guessed, knowing that if he didn't retrieve the salient details, their absence would bug him all day. Closing his eyes again, he concentrated ...

At first all he got was just the impression of whirling angles, that might have been elbows and knees, Jesus spinning on a swastika, a Saguaro cactus with spina-bifida, or all of them. But then with a jolt, which almost detached his head from his spine, it hit him so hard, he recalled a flaming lion that might have been out a medieval bestiary and a liquid black puma, simultaneously launching attacks from both sides, their slashing claws searing the air where he'd just been, as laughing insanely, *(a tactic first learned, fighting playground bullies, who had picked on him because of his hairy legs, which earned him the nickname the Mad Wolf at school)* he dodged into *null space* between triangulated glowing points- a tactic he had relearned, later in life, after studying the habits of the wolf fly.

What was the nightmare about? Was it a ghost attack such as the Contessa wrote of in her aide-de-memoir, after her visit to the maze of forking paths at the Castle? Perhaps to continue his investigations into the applications of the maze schematics, would be to invite an even more deadly attack, when his guard was down, and he slept. For that was no ordinary dream, the cost of energy expended defending himself, had been simply too high for it not to be real at some level. He might have had a heart attack or stroke, an ever-present danger he had learned about, reading medical cases of a doctor in West Africa, where black magic was rife and dream attacks by sorcerers' familiars were common in the dead of the night.

Though only alluded to as the 'unfortunate incident' in the aide-de-memoire, it seems that during the happy couple's stay at the Castle, was cut short when the then Laird, *(Brünhilda's grandfather)* had made improper advances to the Contessa. After they left, a postcard arrived at Haggard thanking the Laird for his hospitality at the castle, and wishing him well. Written in the Count's hand and initialled by his wife, the card had been sent from Aberdeen just before the couple departed to Spitzbergen in a steam ship. In a mad passion of jealous rage at the news, the laird released a phantom black dog he had kept ensnared in the maze for just such a moment – the moment when he renounced women and their wicked ways, for all eternity – or so he wrote later in the Haggard Annals for the year 1902 –

Blissfully unaware a phantom black dog was snuffing their trail, the happy couple continued their summer holiday, taking the dubious sights of the whaling stations in Spitzbergen, skiing down the spine of Norway, before crossing the Baltic and docking at the German port of Lubeck where the Count's footman awaited them with a carriage and horses.

The happy couple were rattling along the cobbled road, somewhere between Rostock and Stettin, when the phantom black dog finally caught up with them.

She wrote later that her phantom wounds sustained fending off the horrible beast still hadn't faded from her arms by upon their arrival in Moscow. Happily they were in time for the much anticipated equinox festivities of the Golden Rite Society, where every year the high and low of Moscow society comingled in a pagan ball, before the Russian Revolution, all those years ago.

But why, Wolfgang wondered, with an effort concentrating on the 'now' again, were the red velvet curtains, heaped in that corner opposite, instead of hanging in the French windows as they should be? No, not possible, he flinched, noticing crude Cyrillic letters inked across the knuckles of a meaty hand poking out the pile. More ink, a snarling bear on a bared midriff, exposed between curtain folds, barbed wire coiled on an extended leg, a death's head tattooed on the back of a shaved head, butted into the corner. This was very bad. Or was he dreaming awake? This, he had read was a relatively common occurrence for dyslexics when highly stressed. Presumably it then it followed he only had to close his eyes, and he would be *dreaming asleep,* rather than *dreaming awake* – and hopefully find himself in a different dream. Then, when he woke up next, the two tattooed goons he'd seen hanging in the street outside the day before, wouldn't be in the room with him, he reasoned.

Wolfgang closed his eyes only to open them, what seemed a minute later, to see ZaZa standing over him.

'Wolfgang, this is just not professional!'

'Ah-hhhm,' he yawned, hugely. Then glancing down, he noticed his dressing gown was open, and gathered it securely about his hairy flanks. 'Sorry, how very unbecoming from an eminent author, etc, etc,' yawning again, he flapped a hand, 'but you've seen it all before my dear.'

'I certainly have now,' she said, archly, turning away to deposit her bag on the Louis XIV. 'Wolfgang, I hope you are...' she stopped midsentence.

'What is it?' he said, dreading what came next.

'You need to tell me what those two men are doing lying wrapped up in the curtains in the corner.

'Oh, are they still there?' Wolfgang said, trying to hide his disappointment, reluctantly looking in the direction of her outsize pointing finger.

'Wolfgang,' she said severely, 'this simply not acceptable. You can't expect me to work with two drunken pals of yours lying in the corner.

'ZaZa, honestly I don't know who they are,' he protested, struggling to get up from his chair. 'Believe me, that's how they were when I woke up earlier.'

'And you left them?'

'I thought I was dreaming and went back to sleep.' Wolfgang said from behind a raised finger, tip-toeing past her desk, and across the last Russian carpet in the house - a fine example of Kirgizstan goat weavers' art - towards the bundled men in the corner.

ZaZa snorted, 'How like a man not to take responsibility. Admit it,' she called loudly to his creeping back, 'you were all partying and they crashed out there!'

So, where are the cans and bottles?' Wolfgang growled back, raising his middle finger back at her, over his shoulder, as he half crouched, looking down at one of the two men, who though insensible, did not appear completely unconscious, he observed, grimly noting a nervous twitch of the yellow crest of a bird, tattooed on the forking branch made by the thumb and index finger of his right hand, splayed by his face – saliva pooled where it had drooled from his lips, one cheek squashed against the boards, milky blue marbles for eyes.

Whatever it was his eyes were still staring at, Wolfgang didn't want to know. However, the vortex that had knotted the pair in the curtains, had known what it was doing, he suspected, amazed at the artful arrangement of legs and arms, even though the curtains binding them seemed to have been considerably stretched in the process. Never mind that mystery, Wolfgang, told himself sternly, as he concentrated on hooking a velvet fold with his toe (he had removed his precious pom-pom slippers for the delicate operation). Only succeeding on his second attempt, when fold fell over the man's face, at last covering those awful staring eyes.

'Horrible,' he murmured, with a satisfying shiver of dread, wondering what this latest Fortean mystery manifesting in his life portended. Slipping his left foot back into its slipper, he resolved that if he survived to the next chapter he would write the adventure up in the annals.

'Well, I am not starting work till they are gone.' Za announced defiantly from behind her desk.

Having recalled when and where he had seen the two men before, Wolfgang retreated from the corner, at least clear in his mind what to do next, 'Give me your foby!' he demanded, snapping the fingers of his extended hand, irritated beyond all measure at this latest interruption *and* the lost time in wages – *Lairds count every cost* is drummed into every bairn from birth, from the popular lullaby every mother in the Kingdom knows -

'There is a service charge of a pound for calls.' She said archly, holding it out.

'Don't worry I'll add it with 2p interest to your next wages,' he snarled resentfully, snatching the foby, thinking if it wasn't for her exorbitant hourly rate he wouldn't have sold the furniture in the first place and now find himself in a criminal master class with the universally feared Systema.

SESSION #5

'Well,' ZaZa said, looking around as she entered the room, 'at least your *friends* are gone from the corner.'

'I told you yesterday I have no idea who those two goons were.'

'Oh, come-on Wolfie,' she said, placing her bag on the Louis XIV next to the laptop, and unbuttoning her coat. 'You seemed to have a very good idea when talking to your *other* friend on my foby.

'John's more of an acquaintance, actually. But yes, he did organize their removal for which I was very grateful.'

'Would that have involved a furniture van and more so called goons?' she said, hanging her coat from the hook on the back of the door.

'Yes, as a matter of fact. They arrived just after you left.'

'And are you expecting any more visitations from friends?' she said smiling broadly, from behind the Louis XIV.

'I sincerely hope not, but you never can be sure what's next.'

'Certainly not with you Wolfgang.' She laughed. 'Now whenever you are ready?' she said, her oversized fingers poised over the keys.

ZARGON, the WICKED SORCERER of the NORTH

by Fanshaw Ramsbowel-Quartz

Chapter 2

*T*he race was on to find a more effective means to dominate the Umbilicals, before the simmering revolt in sectors Y and Z, became a contagion affecting the entire body politic of the North, and the elite class of Cauls also started questioning his right to rule.

Though he didn't yet know the answer, Zargon knew where to look, and what he needed to do to find it. Which was why today the pupils of his big eyes were as wide as saucers, reindeer antlers were strapped to his head, tied to his waist was an apron of snow goose feathers, and he was beating a drum on a high platform raised above the great dome of the Ice House on the top of the world.

'Sevenki, Sevenki, Sevenki,' he chanted, swaying on his haunches, seated cross legged on the platform, while the aurora borealis and the constellations swirled in the night sky about him.

> 'Sevenki, Sevenki, Sevenki
> I implore you,
> Carry me into the
> Great Vortex of the
> Upperworld where
> All secrets of future
> And past are revealed,
> That I may find the
> answer I seek.'

Yes, the great Zargon was an authentic shaman, and getting off his face on reindeer piss or magic lichen - which ever was seasonally available - and beating his drum, was what he did when he didn't know what else to do. Soon his monotonous chanting had the desired effect, and he fell into a trance. In his body no longer, uplifted into the polar vortex created by the rotation of the world, riding his spirit reindeer into the upper realm of the ancestral spirits, where all the secrets of the past present and future are stored.

'Wolfgang,' ZaZa said severely, suddenly, 'This is cultural appropriation.'

'So,' he said, stopping pacing in circles, wearing a track in the soft wool of the Kirgizstan carpet, as he declaimed. 'What do you care?'

'Speaking as an Inuit, I object strongly to you exploiting the myths of my people.'

'You only expose the depths of your ignorance, my dear. Any myths I may have borrowed were from the Evenki of Siberia, and not the Inuit people.'

'It is still cultural appropriation.' She said resentfully.

'So is when non-native speakers use English.'

'That is ridiculous comparison. And you know it Wolfgang.'

'May I resume please?'

'Grudgingly she nodded.

Thank you,' he said, as once more she poised baby zeppelin fingers over the laptop keyboard that seemed tiny in comparison, perhaps explaining her many typos, which of course she denied, claiming it was because she was forced to type phonetically when he was stoned and slurred his words, which of course was most of the time since he chain smoked spliffs, as a matter of course.

In the great vault of the upper sky, Zargon could have learned of amazing cultural achievements of the most recondite civilizations, otherwise lost to history, existing in the pre-diluvian past, but like the other great shaman sorcerers of the

North who had preceded him, he was only interested in instruments of domination, and finding new ways to subjugate the people whom he was pledged to serve.

What he discovered from a mighty civilization, submerged at its zenith some thousands of years before by a great flood, surprised him, for the little device with which that society's often rebellious subjects had been turned into barely more than compliant robots, in a few short decades before their civilization was swept into the dustbin of history, fitted into the palm of his spirit hand.

No matter it was a phantom instrument, he had the schematics for the Tech-cauls to work with, and that was all they needed, to fabricate the little communication devices en-mass for the people, whom, he promised himself, would never

know freedom again, their every thought and action recorded,
to be used against them, as required.

∎∎

Wolfgang was trying to find the number of the new foby he had just purchased with his shrinking wad, after paying ZaZa her exorbitant wages for the week, when a glowing green line, shot down out of the interference pattern in the sky −(which in his ignorance he assumed everyone could see and took to be an everyday part of this new normal branded reality out with the Kingdom) − shafted in between the open french windows, and connected to the foby in his hand, causing it to ring.

'Hells' bells,' he muttered, somehow managing to press the correct button. 'Who the ..?'

'Hello Mate,' a familiar voice said in his ear.

'John, hi, how did you get this number, when I don't even know it?'

'The new boss gave it me just now Mate. Just now.'

'But how did he get it?'

'Nevah moind that mate. Nevah moind. 'E want's to see yew now mate. *Now!*' He repeated, particularly urgently.

'Well, tell him I'm busy.'

'Seriously, yew wouldn't want me to do that mate. Seriously.'

'I am serious. Fuck-him.'

'Lis'en mate,' John said in a hushed tone, 'Yew don't want to tike that attitude, believe me, it's more than yew're loife's worth. These are very 'eavy people mate. Very 'eavy.'

'Look John, don't think I'm not grateful for helping me out the other day with those two goons, but ...'

'Mate, mate, please, we're both in this togethah, an' if yew gow upsetting them more that'll be moi 'ead on the bleedin' block too. Seriously mate, that's w'eah we'll both be mate, on the bleedin' block, mate.'

'Alright, John, if you put it that way,' Wolfgang conceded, being rather impressed by Plain John's use of "Bleedin'." 'What exactly do you want me to do?'

'That's bettah, mate, much bettah. Now, look owt youah window mate, tell me w'ot yew see.'

'A grey limo, longest I've ever seen, parked right across the bus stop, typical rich bastards.' Wolfgang snorted indignantly.

'That's for yew mate, for yew!'

'Really?'

'Yea Mate, I awlready towld yew the boss wants to see yew now, mate. Now!' he insisted.

'Have I got any choice?'

'Na mate,' Plain John replied in a mortally depressed tone, 'wun wiy or anuvvah theah's na escoipe from this lot, mate. Na escoipe at awl.'

BOSSMAN #1

Looking up through the tinted car window, Wolfgang caught a glimpse of the sheer face of a high, black glass tower, as the limo turned into a side entrance and drove down a steep ramp into the basement car park of the building, where two slab faced, big men in dark suits were stood smoking, and obviously waiting.

His nose pressed up against the 200lbs max weight notice, as the tiny lift rapidly ascended, feeling like cheese slice in a fleshy sandwich Wolfgang calculated the combined weight of the two suits, were at least double that, as he imagined the creaking cables breaking and the lift plunging back down to the basement. Supposing he survived the crash, would they then make him walk up all the stairs to the top floor with his legs broken, he wondered?. Of course, they would, what was he thinking, they were Russians, cauterised by centuries of terror and torment, encoded in their DNA, not to mention the more recent legacy of communist gulags, and cannibalism.

Neither had said a word to him, since he stepped out of the limo. In the confines of coffin-like lift, their rank smell was nauseating. An odour of sour crème with a hint of onions, from the one on the right, and pork sausage from the goon on the left. The worst thing however was the pan pipes of a Peruvian band, which was favourite of his wife's, playing from hidden speakers just above as the lift rapidly ascended. The familiar music, reverberating tinnily on the metal walls, reminding Wolfgang of Brünhilda, making him wonder if he would ever see her again.

At the 46th floor, the lift's steel doors slid open on the penthouse suite, which occupied the entire top floor of the tower.

It took all of Wolfgang's inner steel, to stop his knees from trembling as, he crossed what seemed a vast stretch of space, flanked by the two heavies, his every step studied by fit looking, sharp-eyed man behind the sofa, the crystal towers of the City framed in panoramic window at his back, spiking through blanketing clouds under a lattice vapour trails, and city heat haze seamed with static.

'Ah, my good Lord Wolfgang,' the man said, in an accentless, even modulated tone, as they neared. 'So glad you could join me.' He bared his perfect white teeth in welcome, however his dark glittery eyes stayed unsmiling on his broad, otherwise expressionless, face that with its Asiatic cast might have been Mongolian, or Turkoman, Wolfgang supposed, at last gathering his wits together.

Then, when the two men started towards a pair of bronze doors of an elevator, in the wall to the side, Bossman, redirected them back the way they had come, , pointing to the service lift, on the far side of the vast room. *"Smetana Luk, Probka,"* he said sharply. When they didn't move, he added, sharply *'Idi, ya pozvonyu, yesli ty mne nuzhen.'*

'Can you believe it?' he said, to Wolfgang, as they walked away, 'Translated into English their names are Sour Crème Onion and Plug Hole. It is my fate to have inherited them from my Uncle, with this operation. However, I was able to get rid of those responsible for *that* disaster,' with a sweep of his hand, he indicated the huge room behind them, 'before they did more damage.' He shrugged, 'A local team of contractors.'

'It does look a bit of a mess.' Wolfgang said, noticing its clutter for the first time as he watched the two goons who'd steered him across it only a moment before, threading their way around work platforms, between step ladders, under power wires dangling the black squares of missing ceiling panels, and avoiding dust sheets, paint pots, open boxes and their scattered

contents, power tools left where they had been dropped -
everywhere the evidence of hasty departure.

'But what am I thinking of? Pleased to meet you, my name
is Kazen Petrovitch,,' Bossman said formally, extending his
broad hand.

The clasp was cool, firm, dry, a full five seconds, before he
released it, all the while looking Wolfgang in the eyes.

'Actually, I am not a lord, but a laird,' Wolfgang said.

'But it is the same thing, no?' Bosman said, indicating the
sofa to the side.

'Not exactly, Mr Petrovitch, Wolfgang shrugged,, sitting down on one side of the plush sofa, 'I am only a Laird by marriage, and that might not last much longer.'

'Ah, the Lady Brünhilda of the famous Castle Haggard.' Petrovitch said, settling into the chair opposite, his tone implying he knew a whole lot more.

Assuming Petrovich's s mention of Brünhilda, carried an implicit threat, Wolfgang said heavily, 'So, you have been researching my background?'

'I find it pays to learn as much as possible about those we have dealings with. To be perfectly frank, when I heard we have the Laird of Haggard a guest in one of our London houses I could not have been more astonished.'

Wolfgang smiled, 'I hope I don't disappoint you, but Haggard is a pretty minor castle in the Kingdom, at least relatively speaking.'

'Ah, but you are too modest. In Russia we have a saying in a world without rules there are only lords and rascals. This is my castle,' Petrovitch, indicated the penthouse with a sweep of his hand, 'but of your castle, I have heard more than all the others of your country. But what am I thinking of?' He clapped his hands, 'you will take tea, yes? We have all kinds. I can highly recommend the first crop Darjeeling, I have it flown in specially only a few days ago.'

'I'd like that very much,' Wolfgang said, puzzled by Petrovitch's evident interest in Haggard. He had expected to be confronted by a low life gangster a few rungs up the ladder from his goons, but instead, with his courteous manners, and refined tastes, their Boss was clearly even more dangerous than he had supposed.

The tea arrived on a silver tray, with two porcelain cups and saucers, delivered by a slim tall girl, with her chestnut hair gathered up in a bun on the crown of her head, dressed in a demure, pleated, black skirt that reached down to mid-calf and matching blouse with a high ruff, who Petrovitch addressed as Tatiana, before she too was dismissed, though this time in affectionate manner.

'A sweet girl don't you think?' he said, as the bronze doors in the nearby wall, closed behind her, and she departed in the lift by which she had arrived.

'She's your cousin?' Wolfgang said, risking a stab in the dark.

'Good guess!' Petrovitch tapped his temple. 'But much prettier, I think.'

'That is always in the eye of the beholder.' Wolfgang paused, deliberately scrutinising the face before him. He dipped his head. 'But yes, you are right.'

'Ah, you are a teaser. I like that.' For the first time, Petrovitch's smile seemed genuine. 'Now, do you think the tea is brewed long enough?'

Yes, definitely,' Wolfgang nodded, hoping he had at last had reached firmer ground.

ROACH here again ...

Beach Cabin 420, Holiday Inn, Tassiriki Park, Port Vila, Vanuatu, looking out onto the Pacific Ocean.

With more and more countries signing up to the recent international moratorium on flights, at least it's peaceful here, if a bit too clean for my liking. So many germ-free surfaces, does not suit my cockroach sensibilities. Why the world-wide war on bacteria when we owe so much to dirt – having sprung from it? Still, I am enjoying the tranquillity, being the only guest at the Holiday Inn (apart from the insecticide resistant

bugs), the hotel having a full complement of Melanesian staff to service my cockroach needs, which of course are modest.

In town all the banks have closed signs in their windows, so I was relieved to find the UPS office still open, though the nice man I spoke with, was not at all hopeful my package would arrive any time soon, which was a blow. Fortunately, however the tracking number has now turned up on their system, which was good news. Apparently, Wolfgang's coffin is presently stuck on the tarmac in La Paz airport, in Bolivia, so I can only wait for International commercial flights to resume, which could be months, if ever, given growing power of the anti-fossil fuel lobby which increases 10% with every 1cm rise in sea levels – a statistic I read in Newsweek recently. But looking on the bright side, least I know where he now is, which is a positive improvement.

I notice that I made a Freudian slip in penultimate line of the last paragraph, my use of 'he' implying that Wolfgang somehow is not completely dead. What if I find him alive when I finally take delivery of the coffin?

I imagine myself lifting in the lid, passing him a lighted spliff to smoke, and saying 'Don't be a-Freud to be Jung!'

Would he laugh? I wonder. He was always a bit slow at getting my jokes.

BOSSMAN #2

Please, call me Kazen,' Petrovitch said, as he passed Wolfgang a cup of finest Darjeeling tea, saucer. 'People here mangle our Russian names so,' he laughed. 'Of course, you could always try 'the Mad Monk.' His dark eyes glittered.

'Yes, I heard that.'

'From John, yes?'

Wolfgang nodded.

'He *was* a fool.'

'And I am a fool to have believed him when he said your furniture was going to be dumped.' Wolfgang said, wondering if the 'was' indicated Plain John was now past tense, his body encased in a concrete piling in one of the many construction sites in the booming City.

'But that does not mean you are in the clear.' Kazen gestured at the room behind him. 'That old Soviet furniture, would have looked very good here.'

'I can only apologise for what was a genuine mistake.'

'Good, I respect that,' Kazen said, 'It takes a man to own his mistakes. We will find a way for you to make up the loss. I promise you.'

'Not for all of it, surely.' Wolfgang interjected.

'Don't worry,' Kazen smiled indulgently, 'I will not make it hard for you, not like John, who I have discovered abused the trust my uncle placed in him, for quite some time. 'Please, do not give him another thought. But a loss is a loss,' he went on quickly, 'and even a Laird with a fine castle such as yours has to pay.'

'Can I ask you a question, Kazen? Wolfgang said, in a bid to change the subject.

'Whatever you like.'

'This Darjeeling tea is delicious,' Wolfgang held out his empty cup for a refill, 'but, um,' he raised an eyebrow, quizzically, 'Rather, ah, unexpected.'

'And that is your question?'

Wolfgang nodded.

'Ah, you think all we Russians do all day is drink vodka and get drunk.' Chuckling, Kazen poured Wolfgang a second cup.

'Well, it is a popular conception.' Thinking two can play at the grinning game, Wolfgang bared his imperfect teeth.

'Personally, I have not taken alcohol of any kind since I became a monk.'

'So that's true, at least.'

'Yes, before I was obliged to take over the London end of the business, I was seven years with my master who forbade alcohol, except for muscle rubs, and then only after particularly strenuous work-outs. But I have no problem offering it to visitors. For you though,' he shook his head. 'I would not risk it.'

'Why not?'

'After what you did to my soldiers?' Kazen laughed.

'And just what is that supposed to mean?' Wolfgang said, more heatedly, than before.

'The wolf in you overcame their spirit wards.'

'Whatever those wards are, honestly I did nothing.' Wolfgang protested, feeling his face becoming hot.

'The video record shows otherwise.' Kazen smiled, picking up a foby, which had been on the seat beside him. Holding it up he presented the screen to Wolfgang, 'Look, you cannot argue with this.'

'You've been spying on me.' Wolfgang growled, staring at the little screen, and himself, viewed from above, sleeping in the sputnik chair, one side of his face glowing orange from the street light behind the trees outside, in the wind their branches casting moving shadows into the room, as the seconds counted down in the bottom left corner of the screen.

'Nothing personal,' Kazem shrugged.

What am I supposed to be looking at, apart from myself sleeping in my, sorry, *your* chair,' Wolfgang stopped, realising he was slipping back into dangerous territory.

'The house was where my uncle entertained his guests.' Kazem went on after a pause, 'There is total surveillance system in every room, though not in the basement, where we have discovered the cameras have been disabled.'

'Your uncle was blackmailer?' Wolfgang said, connecting the dots.

'He raised it to a high art.' Kazen said almost wistfully, 'It gave him leverage in deals and in the boardroom. And why not? when business is a battlefield, where blackmail, is just one weapon of war. But alas, my uncle's wings turned out to be wax, and he fell, just like his processor before him. It is a lesson I intend to benefit by.'

Kazen leaned around, to check the second counter on the screen of the foby 'Now, pay attention!' he said, tapping a fingernail on the plastic casing, 'or you will miss the moment.'

On the screen, Wolfgang wakes, looks round as a glass pane in the french windows shatters, and a gloved hand reaches in and flips the latch. Wolfgang jumps out of his chair and, in two bounds, crosses the room, appearing to increase in size with each leap, despite putting distance between him in the camera, as two hooded men step in the room from the from balcony outside. One of them aims a high kick, but in a blur of pixels Wolfgang, steps inside the blow, grabs the man by the foot, and hurls him across the room, as though he weighs nothing. Still increasing in size, he advances towards the other man, who retreats into a corner, holding up his hands before his face.

'No way that's me, Wolfgang protests as an interference pattern flashes across the screen and freezes the figures mid-motion, 'He's got to be all of nine feet high, his head bumping the bleeding cornice. Jesus.'

'That's just the transition phase.' Kazen explained, 'I can show you it from another angle, if you like?'

His face pale, for once, speechless, Wolfgang shook his head, for no.

'It was unfortunate the three cameras burned out when they did,' Kazen continued, 'for a moment later you would have seen the Wolf.'

'I still don't believe you.' Wolfgang protested vehemently, pointing a finger at the screen and the monstrous version of himself, towering over the cowering man in the corner.

'You can't argue with the record.' Kazen said, emphatically.

'But assaulting burglars and fighting goes against my pacifist nature.' Wolfgang said weakly.

"A-ha! Now I understand it is to sedate the wolf you smoke hashish so much, and that is why you are so unaware.'

'Unaware of what exactly?' Wolfgang said, it suddenly dawning that Kazen had a complete record of his time in the house, all his dope smoking and sessions with ZaZa, *including* the analmancy, which he forgot to include in his mancy list.

'You stand at the first fork of the path of the Hakim.'

Wolfgang's eyes narrowed, 'Is this by any chance to do with the Maze of Forking Paths at my castle?'

'So!' Kazen clapped his hands. 'You are not completely unaware.'

'Please, I need you to explain.' Wolfgang insisted.

'It is a long story. Where to begin?' Kazen spread the palms of his hands.

'At the beginning?' Wolfgang ventured.

THE **WAY** OF THE **HAKKIM**

T he original Hakkim was a Tungus Shaman of Siberia who passed down the knowledge of the forking paths he had learned from studying the tracks of ravens in snow. His spirit animal was the Bear, though it is said, he could transform himself into an eagle and a lynx with almost equal ease, though that is probably an exaggeration since the expenditure of energy involved in the transition to a different form is enormous, as I think you now know.' Kazen, paused, looking directly at Wolfgang, before continuing.

'But then in the 15th century during the reign of Ivan the Terrible, the Russian Empire expanded into Siberia, and there came the terrible slaughter of the shamans when the secrets of the forking paths were lost. That is, until, the great magus who taught the secrets to the first master of the new line of Hakkim walked the forking paths of your famous maze.'

'Would this be Count Kinsky?'

'Yes, but that was not his real name.'

'What was it?'

'Sergi Putin.'

'Like your president?'

No, he comes later. But Sergi had a famous brother.'

'Let me guess,' Wolfgang leant forwards in his seat, 'Was he by any chance Ras*Putin?*'

Kazen clapped his hands. 'Ah, but you are good at the guessing game. Yes, those Putins were from Ras, a township of Russian settlers in Siberia, all trace of which was erased by order of our dear president, shortly after he was first elected, for reasons that should be obvious, if you think about it.'

'Um, yes,' Wolfgang said distractedly, glimpsing an incoming red streak pass at an acute angle through the tinted glass of the panoramic window, and connect to the mobile in Kazen's hand.

Kazen frowned, looking at the screen, then applied the foby to his ear, 'Da, govorya ... Da ... Net ... Ne peremeshchayte paket ... Podozhdi menya ...' he said, checking the gold Rolex on his wrist, 'Ok ... 15 minut.' Closing his foby with a snap he ended the call. 'My apologies, Lord Wolfgang.'

'Laird.' Wolfgang interjected, smiling.

'Da, Da,' Kazen nodded, other things on his mind, 'Look, I have to go.' He stood up, 'Oh, I almost forget. It is most important you say nothing of our meeting to your Inuit secretary. She is not to be trusted. My advice is get rid of her, ASAP. I explain later, I promise, OK. And no spying I promise. The surveillance is now turned off for guests. We speak soon, wolf to wolf.' He signed foby, forking fingers to his ear, exposing a wolf tattoo on the pale underside of his wrist. Kazen winked,

'I send a car!'

FLASH-BANG!!

Next morning, as hc stood by the French windows, looking out for the 49e bus, and the untrustworthy baggage, Wolfgang wondered how many more amnesiac episodes he'd had over the years. Not counting the recent incident with the goons, he knew of two, however he suspected there could have been more.

The first episode he was aware of occurred after he caught Brünhilda and Mickey inflagrante delicto in the Airstream. Two whole days followed of which he recalled absolutely nothing. Rage, he supposed, since there is nothing like it for burning out brain cells, or so he read once in a Christian scientist pamphlet. Afterwards, he'd checked with friends, but no one remembered seeing him over the two days, nor had there been cash withdrawals in period, when he checked his bank statements, later. Those dates were a complete blank. Then there was the missing 24 hours, he'd never been able to account for on one of his trips to the R.U. economic zone in the south of the Kingdom. At the time, he'd put the episode down to a date slip, that being a leap year, and confusion born of his dyslexia, however he now saw that was just a story he told himself to cover up something much more disquieting.

Who was running the show, his inner wolf or himself, he wondered? Or were they both the same? Anyway, he'd always considered himself to be a bit of a lone wolf, so perhaps the fork of Hakkim which Kazen spoke of, was the point, indicating he should accept his inner wolf, and bring it back into the warmth of the fold. But folds were where sheep were kept, so that was probably a very bad idea indeed. But, ultimately, was he a sheep or a wolf? It wasn't a question, when he thought about it. He'd choose wolf any day. More than his name, it was his nature, as demonstrated by his hairy flanks and paw-like feet. But that aspect of him had never been accepted by Society. At his stepmother's instigation, he had been put in a cage at school, until he gave a good enough pretence of conforming. And later, marriage had turned into another straightjacket. All too soon Brünhilda's early fascination in his hairy lower half had waned, her evident disinterest concealing a deeper aversion, which he suspected was a primeval herd hatred of everything to do with wolves. Or perhaps more accurately, the ancient hatred of conformist sheep for their beastly lower halves. Well, which ever way that was, and whatever the risks involved, it was imperative he must release his inner wolf, for to do otherwise would be to imperil the most precious part of him – years out in the cold craving affection, starved of company – the need all creatures have for their kind – Perhaps that was why, despite his fuck-up selling the Sputnik furniture, he and Kazen got on so well? Their inner wolves recognised each other. Yea, that was it, he was sure. Somehow he'd find away to repay him. One thing that still puzzled him however, was Kazen's almost mystical fascination with the maze of forking paths, which after all had been designed by a former Laird, with the intention of trapping those few poachers who had managed to evade the other defences, protecting the Castle's vegetable garden, when Haggard was under siege by starving peasants during the hungry years of ...

Suddenly, out of the corner of his eye, he glimpsed a livid green/ red streak entering the room at a low angle through the French windows. A heartbeat later, somewhere nearby a phone rang. Feeling an accompanying vibration in his groin, Wolfgang looked down, and realized the ringing was from his new foby device, which he had forgotten was in his trouser pocket.

'Hello..?' he said tentatively.

'Wolfgang!' the familiar voice of his lawyer, blared in his ear.

'Jaws, how good of you to call.' He said holding the foby away from his ear, as it had just occurred to him that the green and red signal might harm his brain.

'Well, at least you sound well, considering you are on the missing person's register *and* since yesterday there is an international arrest warrant out for you.' Jaws went on.

'You are serious?'

'Absolutely dear chap. But that was clever to leave the Kingdom when you did. The police have been hunting high and low for you ever since.'

'Why?

'Rather inconveniently your fancy slippers will keep turning up at the sites of unexplained deaths ...'

'Unexplained?' Wolfgang interjected.

'Yes, dear chap, there is some doubt about the common cause, however, I am advised that the Police are now treating them as murders ...' He paused, 'hello, are you still there?'

'I'm listening,' Wolfgang said after a moment, 'Go on.'

'From what I understand, all the victims were heavy drug users.'

'You don't believe I've anything to do with these, um,' Wolfgang hesitated, 'unexplained murders.'

'No, no dear chap, absolutely not. Howevah, my considered advice is for you to keep your head down until the whole thing blows over.'

'How did you get this number?'

'Best not to ask dear chap.'

'Just as long as the boys in blue don't find I'm in ...'

'Don't say it, dear chap,' Jaws interjected, hastily. 'That way I can honestly say I don't know, if asked again.'

'You've already talked to the police?'

'Yes, yes, an Inspector Hackett. He even claims you escaped from a secure mental ward some years ago. Total nonsense, of course.'

'So, it's serious.'

'Well, you will keep getting into scrapes, dear chap. But, as I say, keep the old head down, and all will blow over.'

'I will Jaws, I promise. Before I go, any news on the divorce front?'

'Kicked into the long grass, more precisely the High Court of Family Arbitrage, all because I invoked the precedent of

Gilbert versus Cunningford, an obscure case heard by the notorious judge, Lord Jeffries, in the Crown Appellant Court, which of course was disbanded in the reign of ...'

'Spare me the details,' Wolfgang cut him off, knowing if he allowed Jaws to continue a second longer, next he would be giving his latest theories on the Great Prelapsarian Schism of 1744, an obsessive subject for Jaws, who believed an ancestor of his had been cheated out of a great fortune by a Bishop involved in the Conspiracy.

'All you need know is it'll take years dear chap. Decades if needs be.'

'Just what I wanted to hear Jaws. Meanwhile, I don't suppose there are now available funds you could release?

'Ah, but then I would need an address, wouldn't I? And don't suggest a third party, or offshore bank account number, or a security box, because those would still compromise me as your lawyer, and might even lead me to being disbarred, in which case I could be on no further service to you. It pains me to say this, but unfortunately, until the storm blows over, you are on your own dear chap.'

So, that was the way the cookie crumbled, the land lay, the wind blew, and the rats skipped the ship, Wolfgang thought gloomily, as he stood looking out on the french windows at the passing traffic, on the road below. Discounting Plain John, who one way or another was now past tense, only Zaza and of course Kazen knew where he was, so at least he had that small crumb of comfort, with which to reassure himself.

As for the murders, if that is what they were, he didn't want to know any details, particularly the names and dates. The Kingdom drug sub-culture was small, so it followed that the chances were high he'd have known one or more of the victims. And if the dates of the murders - so called, matched his amnesiac episodes. What then? His inner wolf would never be able to endure imprisonment in the Rig B, and 20 years looking out on the lonely sea from the porthole of his cell, which of course he would have to share with another prisoner, who was probably violent, unlike himself and might even be a serial killer. Since he didn't want to have to murder himself - ie commit suicide - his only rational choice was permanent exile. Wolfgang's shoulders slumped at the prospect of never seeing his castle again.

Where was he? Oh yea. London. standing between open French windows, looking out for his secretary onto the tree lined street.

Still no sign of the 49e bus, yet ... But no, he was wrong, he realized, spotting it coming round the next street corner, but then, instead of pulling up at its stop below, the red bus continued towards the towers of the city, looming out of the city smog in the distance. This was not like the baggage to miss her bus, for although Zaza was unreliable in most departments, bad time keeping was not among them.

Thinking of calling Jaws, for no other reason than hearing a friendly voice, Wolfgang was turning away from the window when a heavy bass beat from outside drew his attention back to the window. The headache inducing thudding seemed to be issuing a shiny black BMW car, which looked like it was pumped up on steroids, with flaring wheel arches, fat tyres, air gills on the sides, and double barrel chromium exhausts, parked-up with two wheels on the narrow pavement across the road.

Although a latecomer to City life, Wolfgang was well aware that BMWs were the car of choice for black drug dealers, giving the marque its street name of Black Man's Willie. But no, this prick mobile was a WMW, Wolfgang reconsidered, catching a glimpse of a shiny white pate behind the partially open driver's window as, on the far side of the car, the passenger door opened, and ZaZa stepped out onto the pavement. Then the driver's window scrolled down, and lo and behold, there was Skull, grinning back up at him. Their eyes met, then still holding the foby, Wolfgang made a warding gesture with both hands, as Skull pointed pistol fingers out of his window, and mouthed 'Bang!' Simultaneously, the foby which Wolfgang was fumbling, flashed.

Unsure just exactly what had just occurred, Wolfgang stepped backwards, into the room, of sight from the road, stared at his foby, and Skull, captured on the screen, pointing pistol fingers out of his car window, his bony face a rictus of hatred.

Unbelievable, Wolfgang thought, so these foby devices take photos too. Was, Kazen watching even now, through the hidden cameras of the house's surveillance system, he wondered, but if so, did that matter anyway? Was there any end to the uses of fobys? Still staring at the image he then realized he had Skull bang to rights, and a way out of the RAS contract with his untrustworthy amanuensis. Fortunately in his perusal of the document –he had noticed a clause concerning harassment, and intimidation by third parties. Skull's reappearance in his life, he realised, was ever a spur to action, marking another fork in the road. This time, dyslexia not withstanding, he was resolved to write the next volume in his magnum opus, all by himself, and if that meant he had to walk on broken glass, so be it.

With big thanks to my fellow creatives for the images which I sourced on Creative Commons. If you wish to be mentioned by name on future editions, please contact me at will@inkistan.com.

INKISTAN
.COM

More Novels by Will Lorimer, published by Inkistan.com

TRANSEND
Before the Fall

As the Man said, 'It's our job to ensure the END has a time-table ... Events must be controlled. We can't just bow down to the inevitable!' The clock is ticking. Preparations are complete. Mountain refuges have beenprepared for those with sufficient funds.

After the Fall ---

There's the CEO's billionaires, and Politicians living extended lives under the Mountain, whose status has been reduced to that of mere numbers.
There's the Punk saboteur, and her orange fireball sidekick, causing mayhem under the Mountain.
There's the fattest girl in the world who one day willbe queen.
There's No. 1 and No. 3 in lockdown in a safe room, wondering what's going in the corridors beyond.
There's the phosphorescent dust thick in the air,which gets into everything, even miles underground.
There's the sclerotic eye which wanders the sky and beams down pestilence on the land below.
There's Bonaparte, only he's black – in charge of the Consensus, who thinks he rules the world.
There's the war between the Consensus, and the Trans-human rebels, as an even more precipitous Fall,looms.

ASIN: 1911289543 – (paperback) ASIN: B00WPV0E6M (KINDLE)

ON THE RUN IN DREAMTIME
(Two editions, one illustrated)

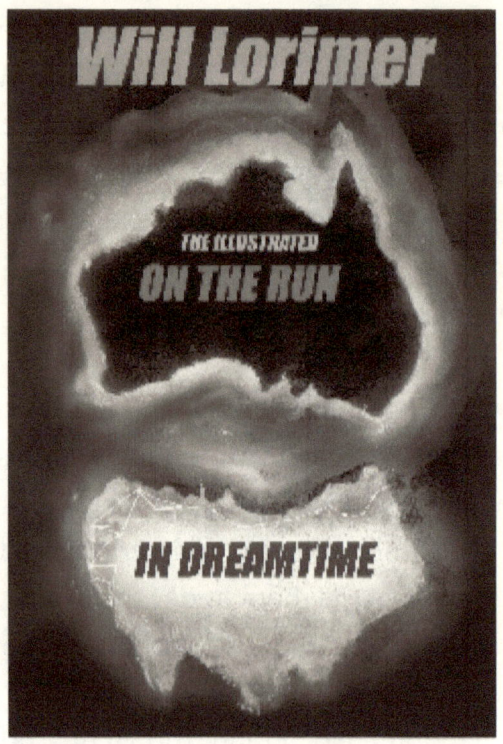

The unlikeliest duo you'll encounter within the covers of a book or otherwise, Lobo and Frankie are the natural successors to Don Juan, and Carlos Castaneda, with a pinch of Laurel and Hardy for good measure. Lobo is a Swiss-Tibetan-playboy-mystic, who believes that Frank is the Chosen One. A pity then that the Chosen One should turn out to be a lazy, dirty mouthed Scotsman with as much mental clarity as a guinea pig, but Lobo is not deterred. Together they blaze an unstoppable trail across an unsuspecting Australia, in a pristine white falcon UTE – cruising the highways, sneaking

ON THE RUN IN DREAMTIME

Two men on the run, a Tibetan who has no need of sleep or money,
and his 'chosen one', a Scotsman fleeing his vengeful wife and a past
he wants to forget, blaze a trail through Dreamtime and Oz in a stolen car.

Will Lorimer is the author of four novels,
all of which are available on Amazon.

On The Run In Dreamtime

Will Lorimer

*two men in a fast car
when roads were free*

Will Lorimer

the byways, and syphoning off gas pretty much everywhere. From the dives of Kings Cross Sydney, to the wild wastes of flying doctor country, they connive, conspire, and con their way in and out of trouble, in scenarios that Lobo creates to demonstrate the secret teachings of his master in a cave, back in Tibet. Along the road they encounter the gay queen of Melbourne, the gorgeous Renaldo Monte-Video, Nazis hiding out in a Queensland banana plantation when not on the Moon, fat necked outback cops, an aborigine-trans-rights activist, lesbian truckers, hookers and frustrated housewives of the outback.

ASIN: 1838138250

INCOMPARABLY NARRATED   BY THE AUTHOR

THE LAST OF THE LUTCHENS
(two editions, one illustrated)

the
Last of the
Lutchens

THE ILLUSTRATED EDITION

Will Lorimer

Britain over the last hundred years, through the eyes of an Anglo-Scots family of dubious lineage, featuring the illusions and obsessions of three generations of the Lutchens, woven together in a genealogical tree rooted in a Scotland which we only thought we knew. Starting in the swinging sixties as the Beatles' first single tops the charts and the Cuban Crisis looms, the narrative tracks back through two world wars to uncover a skeleton in the family closet, before proceeding full circle, to when a national crisis threatens to break-up the disunited family.

Will the Lutchens go their separate ways, or patch up their differences? Everything hangs in the balance for the family, and also the British nation state.

ASIN: 0956957730

THE ESCAPE FROM MICTLÁN TRILOGY
(an overview)

It was a secret from his amnesic past that even his NY analyst couldn't decipher, which meant he had to go to Mexico in search of answers, specifically to a ghost town in the bandit-infested Sierra Madre, where his mother was waiting for him at the only hotel in town.

In the depths of the Sierra Madre, behind a tunnel carved through the top of a mountain, one of the five that surrounded the place like the fingers of a hand, is the strangest ghost town in Mexico. There's a hotel, run by a serial killer, and just across the street, a cantina, run by a drug cartel banker. The town was founded in 1495, after the fall of Tenochtitlán, when a band of thirteen conquistadores hunting the last Aztec eagle warriors in the mountains, discovered silver in the ashes of the previous night's fire. Descendants of the conquistadores ruled the town for four hundred years, which became the richest in Mexico, with a treasury, a mint, even an opera and of course a magnificent cathedral, until Pancho Villa and his North Division took the town in 1914, and executed the surviving members of the thirteen ruling families, who took the location of the fabulous treasure, to their graves.

After the Revolution, adventurers, attracted by the legend of the Treasure of the Sierra Madre (some said that there were thirteen treasures), dynamited the majority of the buildings of the medieval town — but of the treasure, or treasures, nothing was ever found.

The indigenous Nahuatl tribes of the remote mountains believe the treasure will never leave the town because it is the property of the Lord of Death, king of Mictlán, and whoever discovers its location will be taken to one of the nine levels of the vast kingdom, which lies under the buried silver mines, below the town with no name, hidden behind a long tunnel, cut through a mountain peak high in the remote sierra Madre, somewhere in Mexico.

This is the story of a search for answers, among which is what happened to a disgraced bishop, a enormously wealthy Kabbalist, damned for his many crimes, who departed this life for Mictlán with the secret of the treasures, where his bastard son has to follow, is he is ever to discover decipher the riddles of amnesic past.

BOOK 1

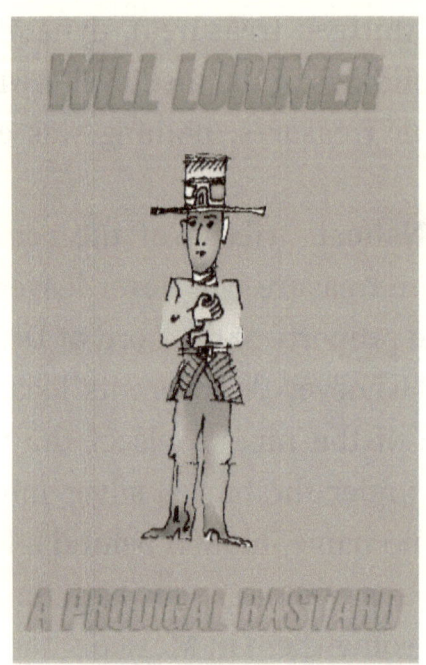

A prodigal bastard searching for his missing father, a Catholic bishop, instead finds his mother managing the only hotel in the Mexican town with no name, where nothing is as it seems, every day is the Day of the Dead, and the cathedral bells toll 13 at midnight. Even the Police chief has fled following the discovery of a mass grave under the bandstand in the main square, and the only safe place in town is the local cantina, where the barman is the narco-cartel banker. Based on the author's real-life experiences in the remote Sierra Madre of Mexico, A Prodigal Bastard is the first book of the Escape From Mictlan Trilogy. The novel is illustrated with drawings by the Author, many of which are from the year he spent trying to escape from the Town with no name.

ASIN: 1838138226 ASIN: B08DXX9WF4

BOOK 2

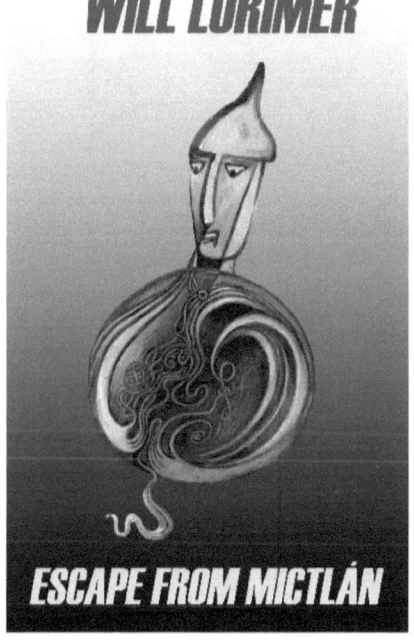

A Prodigal bastard's search for his father continues, from the Town with No Name, over the last unmapped mountain range in Mexico, to the Narco HQ, in ahidden canyon, and eventually, into Mictlan, where he finally gets some answers to the questions bugging him ever since the philandering catholic bishop ran out on his life, when he was only 5 years old. Next he has to getout of Mictlán, and his job as the ferryman transporting the dead across the Black River.

ASIN: B08DXX9WF4

ASIN: B08FG9JWN7

BOOK 3

A prodigal bastard returns in a disembodied
state to the Town with No Name.

Next, he must recover his body, if he is to ever
to escape to the world outside.

ASIN: 1838138226

The Spanish language edition of the Escape
from Mictlan Trilogy, in one illustrated Volume.

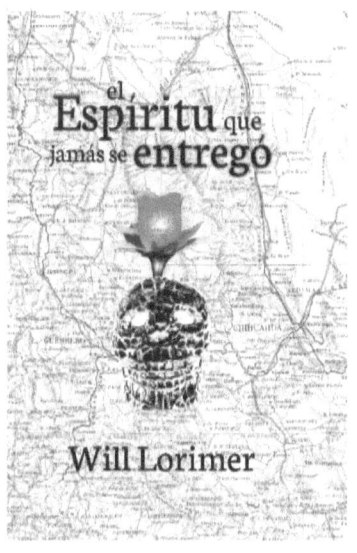

Se trataba de un secreto de su pasado amnésico que
ni siquiera su analista de N. Y. era capaz de descifrar,
lo que significaba que tenía que ir a México en busca
de respuestas, específicamente a un pueblo fantasma
en la Sierra Madre, infestada de bandidos, donde su
madre lo esperaba en el único hotel del pueblo. En lo
recóndito de la Sierra Madre, tras un túnel tallado a
través de la cima de una montaña, una de las cinco
que rodeaban el lugar como los dedos de una mano,
está el pueblo fantasma más extraño de México. Hay
un hotel, administrado por una asesina en serie, y
justo cruzando la calle, una cantina, administrada
por el banquero de un narco-cartel. El pueblo fue
fundado en 1495, cuando una banda de
conquistadores que, tras la caída de Tenochtitlán,

habían estado cazando en las montañas a los últimos guerreros águila aztecas, encontraron plata en las cenizas del fuego de la noche anterior. Eran trece conquistadores, cuyos descendientes gobernaron el pueblo por cuatrocientos años, el más rico de México en su momento, con una tesorería, una casa de moneda, incluso una ópera y por supuesto una catedral, hasta que Pancho Villa y su División del Norte tomaron el pueblo en 1914 y fusilaron a los descendientes de los conquistadores, quienes se llevaron a la tumba la locación del tesoro secreto. Terminada la Revolución, una serie de aventureros, atraídos por la leyenda del Tesoro de la Sierra Madre (algunos decían que había trece tesoros), dinamitó la mayoría de los edificios del pueblo medieval—pero del tesoro, o tesoros, nada nuncase supo. Los nahuas de las remotas montañas piensan que jamás se sabrá, pues es propiedad del Señor de la Muerte, rey del Mictlán, y quien descubra su locación será llevado a uno de los nueve niveles del vasto reino, que yace bajo las minas de plata sepultadas en las montañas. Esta es la historia de una búsqueda de respuestas, entre las cuales está lo que le pasó a un obispo deshonrado, un maldito cabalista enormemente rico, que partió al Mictlán con el secreto de los tesoros, a donde su hijo bastardo tiene que ir, si es que quiere descifrar los enigmas de su pasado amnésico.

ASIN: 1548139157

WOLFGANG

Book 1 Beware of the Dog)
(The short life and times of WOLFGANG, Laird of
Castle Haggard)

Illustrated by the author

Enfant terrible, a freak of nature. His rise from obscurity to become the Laird of Castle Haggard, following his marriage to Lady Brünhilda Constanze Haggard. His travails restoring the Castle. The strange customs and traditions of the Castle. Beset by demons disturbed by his renovations – a black dog, the Red Duchess, and vengeful ghosts. Betrayed in love - a laird cuckholded. The laird's war against a drug baron and his henchmen. An encounter with Lucifer in a black pit. The riddle of the laird's map of shifting lines and the mystery of the forking paths of the Castle's famous vegetable garden. All this and more recounted in a series of tales, dictated to the laird's secretary, an untrustworthy Inuit, who has an even greater capacity for drugs than the laird himself, which is saying something.

ASIN: 1838138242

DOG DAYS IN NEW YORK

SHORT STORIES OF MANHATTAN FROM
BEFORE THE FALL

WHO'S ART?

PICTURE POEMS #1

1980-2020

WILL LORIMER

Every picture tells a story and every poem is a picture in this travelogue through the mind of the artist charting the absurdities, follies, and delusions of our troubled times. ASIN: 1838138269

MEET THE AUTHOR

To discover more of Will's multi-media Art –
Books, videos, glass works, paintings & etc

Take a trip to Inkistan

INKISTAN
.COM

www.ingramcontent.com/pod-product-compliance
Lightning Source LLC
Chambersburg PA
CBHW021155130626
46554CB00005B/1836